Blood Red

JIM ARCHER

lettertec

For my wife Veronica

and

son Patrick

ABOUT THE AUTHOR

Jim Archer was born in "The Mystery House" in French's Quay in Cork City during the harsh winter of 1947. After attending the nuns at St Mary's of the Isle he was educated by the Presentation

Brothers at Colaiste Chriost Ri. Sport was the big thing in his life - hurling and football, sprinting and long jumping.

After publishing short stories in "The Cork Weekly Examiner" he went on to write scripts and short drama that were staged in The Cork Opera House in the seventies.

He continued to write on and off over the years – poetry, short stories, humourus articles for print and radio.

Having lived in London and Paris he eventually settled down in Dublin and is married to Veronica and has one son Patrick.

Blog: jimarcherscribblerand.com

Email: jimarcherscribblerand@gmail.com

Jim Archer: Introduction

I was in school with Jim Archer. This in itself may not be of shattering significance as there were many of us there. We did what we had to do being wrapped up in ourselves and gagging to go forth into the world. None of us had the least clue what would befall us as we set out into the light.

There were different gangs of us, as there always is, when we were in school. Some of us inclined towards debates and the arts and music, and might have done some good. But the public face of the school was in football, hurling and other sports, this was where we could beat the world, or even Cork, which was more or less the same thing.

Every one of us carries a different memory of our time in school, and of those who were our mates. There was he who defied the teacher, the guy who spilled the acid in the lab, the chancer who sang out of tune to piss the choir off, the *buachaill* who brought the frog in…

My abiding memory of Jim Archer was in a college game against I don't remember who, but I think it was in Fermoy. He plucked a high ball out of the air, clutched it to his chest, hugged it for a moment, did a little shimmy, turned on a farthing, rounded his marker, and lofted the ball over the bar. I saw it many times afterwards. It was done with ease, with grace, and with aplomb, whatever that latter word means.

Most of all, it was done with passion. Hurling and football allows a certain space, you can breathe in the gaps. Not so, the mad sport of sprinting. A sprint is a bullet from a gun, a rocket from the earth, an ejaculation from what lies beneath. If Jim rounded backs and follied forwards in hurling and football his path in athletics was a *líne dhíreach*, a straight line to the finish. I may be wrong, but I don't think a faster sprinter ever emerged from Colàiste Chríost Rí.

He had a barreled body, round on top, and to us, spindly below. How those pared-down legs could transport an upper body of muscle and bone with such alacrity was never explained in our physics classes. He was a bolt from the line, a flash through the pan, a dart from the depths, and damn them all. He was our Bob Hayes and Enrique Figuerole, and I suppose a few years later he would have been our Jim Hines or our Lennox Miller, forgotten now, but flaring then. As an athlete, a hurler and a footballer, he had done it all.

This book was a journey for me, as it will be for everybody else. What happens to us when we leave school? School is a haven in which we are hemmed in by the necessities of the moment, of time tables, of events, of exams. That future beyond is not a world which we have even imagined. Where do we go to, our lovelies, when we have abandoned our beds? This is one answer, a human, witty, self-deprecating, fully-confident, non-bullshitting, adventuresome, at times scary, otherwise amusing, always engaging, occasionally hilarious, shot through with humanity tale of life and love and pain and survival and hope.

While this itch to know what happened a colleague in those years after school was personal for me, it has a resonance for everybody else also. It is the story of everyman and everywoman. Autobiography is shot through with what might have been, the roads not taken in that wood, the whole forked rivulets of happenstance. But there is also that other voice: the sense that it couldn't ever have been otherwise, that this was what that old whore destiny had stacked up.

Jim Archer could, of course, have taken other roads. Some of them would have been dull and boring. But it is unlikely he would have suffered them gladly. Life explodes in too many of these pages and his personality burbles to be heard. His sojourn in Paris as a young man living in dodgy hotels, driving in mad traffic without sufficient knowledge and hanging out with dubious women from other parts of the world could, no doubt, have been replicated in some fashion if he had taken off to other cities. Even in Cork some of it might have happened but without the weather and the exoticness. But yet, a particular Paris, at a particular time, for a particular young man comes alive and we wallow in it, as he certainly did.

It was the Irish writer Máirtín Ó Cadhain who once said that a deep Irish trait was the admixture of fun with seriousness. This is a book rife with tragedy and comedy mashed together. This may be best illustrated where he suffers a serious accident, breaking his ankle and displacing bones, requiring a long stay in hospital. Remember that here is a serious athlete, a sprinter who burst from the blocks, somebody who challenged the bestest speed of the rest of us plaited together. By a silly unfortunate chance, he is laid low.

Yet these four months in hospital show the humour and humanity breaking through. There is the character called 'Compensation' because all he can think of is how much money could be filched from an accident. We have all met him. The Hitler nurse who brooked no breaking of rules. We have met her too. More tragically the Echo Boy who was really a man whose screams of pain seared through the ward. More comically the smuggling and guzzling of bottles of forbidden Guinness, and then the Mummy, the Stud, the Smiley and others. But the chapter ends with an old man from the country who is brought in and Jim fills his pipe of tobacco for him - as it happens - for the last time. The old man turns over and dies. He writes a poem, stunning in its simplicity, huge in its love of other people, and of this man in particular whom he never knew. It is not a bad emblem for the entire book.

To those of us who ever worked in a summer job on a factory floor and survived the mechanical repetition, a job in Fords would have been Limbo on earth. Jim worked in Fords as did at least one father of some child in every classroom in Cork city. He was fortunate in having office work and being able to observe what was going on with some detachment. Despite the braindumbing work for many, the crack was mighty, as it had to be in order to survive. Again, the place was replete with 'characters': The Cock who yodeled a cock-a-doodle when he could to piss people off, the black American interloper with the exotic name of Luther, the cook called Flintstone who was proud of his gungy gudge glob, the dapper Den who knocked down a wall partition just to release a cat from the premises, and of course, the blonde bombshell who exceeded the rules of the most skimpy miniskirts which had just come into vogue and who was given the appropriate name of 'Mortal Sin.' It was a name which meant a lot then, but very little now.

One of the great themes of the story is that of health. One might have thought that this shouldn't be. He was the healthiest specimen around, bursting with energy, blazing with drive, burnished with all the futures. And yet, there were ways in which he was dealt a bum hand. He lists at one stage, this excluding earlier accidents and mishaps, 'genetic gout, peptic ulcer, four operations on my hands and feet, high blood pressure, high cholesterol, eye migraine, liver failure and now a fucking heart by-pass'. Yet there is no moaning at the bar before he sets out on the next medical adventure. He repeats with some comfort the old saw: 'If you were born to be hanged, you can go to sea in a bucket and you won't be drowned.' Not very scientific, you might say, but what has science got to do with it?

Before his big operation he went through the whole gummed up gamut of reveries of youth on the Lee Fields with his father, and the thought of what he had achieved already, and his loving wife and growing-up son, and the daffodils that would be blooming when he woke up, and the rabbits, and the grass, and the smell of the spring in the morning early. It is this switch from the ordinary and normal to the vulnerable and touching which marks the book as being a fluent testament to the human spirit in all its streaky guises.

And, oh, yes, he made an eejit of himself too, 'cos don't we all? There was one mad single gambling hilarious-in-hindsight episode in which instant grounded sense won the day, then more hairy stuff, even a personal trainer. Yet there was always a solid wall of cop on. Maybe this is just what life gives you if you wish to embrace it. Maybe too, the fact that he was a superb athlete and a brilliant hurler and footballer knocked whatever crap could be ingested in a more refined atmosphere from him.

Coláiste Chríost Rí was one of the most successful secondary schools of its time and place. Jim was one of most luminarious who starred on the sporting fields. But we also did debating in Irish and in English and swept before us, plays by classical and by contemporary authors, and musicals, and popular operas, and had bands and musical ensembles. Was there any other school in Ireland that produced plays by Gogol or by John Arden in our time, even when he was then ardently under suspicion as an awful socialist? In fact, it is very difficult to think what we did not have. We had a film society when we thought fillum was just about cowboys and Indians. We were told it was an art form, and resisted our teachers' claims until we knew better.

Our own very small class pupped up two people who held university chairs and became members of the Royal Irish Academy, two other university lecturers (who would be known fancifully as professors in the US), a prize-winning film maker and broadcaster, at least one professional actor, a radio producer of arts programmes, a high-ranking civil servant, a champion dancer, and innumerable engineers and business people about whom we know very little. I know of at least two who made a stack of money meaning millions, although one of them admitted that he had lost most of it too. There were sports stars and hack artists and those who might have made it. Those who played corner back and never won a medal, like me.

Whatever anyone did is sad success in the crassly worldly sense. This crass worldly sense means nothing ultimately. Our class and classes did our own thing and things. Everyone was a success, or not, in his own way. Living, loving and laughing is a great heritage. This memoir is only one of all the others that could have been written delineating the world we lived in, and the world we made. If written, they might not be as sassy and as adventurous as this is. Everybody's story reached out around Ireland and wherever else. Not bad really for one Leaving Certificate class of 1965. Writing without bitterness and with stark bald realism as this memoir does is a testament of his and our own gutsy survival, much just luck, much down to individual pluck.

Jim Archer's saga is part of those kindergarten years for the school, but also part of those halcyon days for Cork hurling when we just expected to win everything, and just part of the story of a young man growing up, reaching maturity of a kind, suffering more than most's share of the slings and arrows of bad health, and winning out with courage, with conviction and with good spirit. It is that good spirit that we take with us after reading this rambunctious memoir.

No book is worth reading unless it has some sense of style. Jim has honed his with wit and with sharpness. It is poetic at times, plain when needed, descriptive as it goes, witty all along. But there is always a surprising turn of phrase – 'More attachments than a Dyson vacuum cleaner', 'More cures in his name than Padre Pio', 'Inside every good man is a miserable bollocks', '(brain) revolted like a South American general' and so on, for what is writing without wit? It is dull and boring. There is nothing dull and boring about this tale of adventure, of love, of pain and of courage. It is his story, but in another sense it is the story of our time.

It is also a story of Cork and of its beyond, the Cork diaspora which goes away but never leaves. Rebel Cork flows in the inky veins of this life-enhancing biography, not the stupid rebel Cork of those two muddied pissed-upon streets when the arse-artist Perkin Warbeck landed to claim the throne of some other blood stained escutcheon nobody seeking the English throne, but the far more real rebel Cork of the war of independence winning freedom for most of the country. He does not hide this lineage throughout his tale, and why should he? In these coming years, we will be in great need of it when the shades of shame will attempt to smother what has been achieved.

This is a book of warmth and of width, of wit, of wonder and of wander. It is a book written on its own terms, revealing to those who know the author, but even more revealing to those whose paths he never crossed.

Alan Titley

Schoolmate 1960-65

CRADLE - Jim Archer

Divided Old River Lee

You held us together

Your streams – our dreams

Trapped in old ways

You left us to create our Gods from within

Ringey, Holy Joe, Andy Ga.

Our tribe admired genius

Respected egits

For we all drank from the same mad chalice

With Bishops, Priests and Mercy Nuns.

Divided Old River Lee

You flowed in our veins through blood red hearts

You sent passions cascading like our voices

Lilting singing cursing crying breathing

Dying

Entombing the past.

Finally to awake to see silver droplets

Riding clouds above Goughane.

Oh our new waters – our new dreams

Rushing out to Roches Point

And beyond to Sargasso Sea

CHAPTER ONE

When I awoke on the morning of my fortieth birthday I suddenly realised that I had not died a young man. This thought stayed with me for a few days, until a bigger realisation struck me, that for all those long forty years, I had achieved very little in my life. Putting aside the fact that I once ran the 100 metres in the sixties against three of the world's greatest sprinters ; there was the world record holder Charlie Green; Mel Pender – a man who won a hatful of Olympic Gold Medals; the third was the then current world champion De Blanc. This career highlight achieved by very few Irishmen in their lifetimes did little to ease my plight.

This was chicken feed to someone with an ego as big as mine. I had a list of ambitions as long as your arm since early childhood, and now, arriving at this important juncture in my life, told its own story to me. Over the next few weeks, I tried my best to remain optimistic, but I have to admit that I was panicking in no small way. Trying the impossible task of fusing the past, the present and the future all into the one moment by a panicky man can be a daunting and frightening experience.

Bit-by-bit, it was dawning on me that I was forty and fucked!

Now, burdened with the dual characteristics of being bald and fat – the two most dreaded words for a middle aged male to embrace – and added to this if you don't mind, a pervasive little bastard called gout was finding lodgings in my big toe. Put in the mix the occasional chest pain; the high cholesterol; the high blood pressure; and not forgetting the ever-expanding stomach reaching for the ground, and I'm pretty sure that a certain picture is emerging, that I was not the healthiest specimen on the planet. So, my team of doctors, after a lengthy meeting, advised me to quit work and close my business, and my wife bought me a word processor to keep me out of Grange Gorman.

From the centre of Croke Park, I had moved into Hill Sixteen, in a metaphorical sense. Over the next couple of weeks I was in deep mourning; for the loss of my good health; for letting my family down; for letting my ambitions slide into oblivion; plus all the misgivings I had about my health and finances for the future. For Christ sake, I was one of the most active and gifted sportsmen of my generation. I was an all-round athlete at school, winning titles in both sprinting and long jumping. I played hurling and football for five years for the school team at Colaiste Chriost Ri, in Cork, and even had the great honour of captaining the senior hurling team in the Harty Cup. Allied to this, I played hurling and football for all the under-aged Cork teams, and was a regular member of St. Finbarrs hurling and football senior teams while still in my teens. Through immaturity and hot-headedness, I retired from GAA following an argument at the ripe old age of nineteen, but, I quickly established myself as one of the leading sprinters in Ireland, almost instantly. So it was no idle thought, to say that I was a pretty good sports person. And I never let up. After my athletic career was over, I spent lunchtimes bathed in sweat, skuttering squash balls, left, right and centre, and pounding into ice-cold tubs and saunas round Dublin, in one almighty effort to keep my fitness, if not my youth intact. But all the sweat and endeavour was in vain. I would have been as well off skulling Cote de Rhone in seedy lap dancing joints, until early morning. I was a goner from the outset. My defective genes, with their precision watches, had other ideas. The relevance of my Grandmother's words each day became a deeper truth for me.

"If you are born to be hanged, you can go to sea in a bucket and you won't be drowned."

I looked round me, and the evidence of that statement was all too plain to be seen. I was having a pint in my local pub in Cork, on one of my spiritual visits, and minding my own business. This guy was sitting some seats away from me, and was looking in my direction, as if he knew me. He smiled over and I returned the smile out of good manners. With that, he left his seat, and came up to me.

"Are you Jim Archer?" He spoke with a half-cockney accent.

I own up.

"Haven't seen you for donkey's years."

"Jes, how are things?"

I was stumped. I hadn't the foggiest notion who he was.

"Remember me? I'm Jerry Murphy from around the corner. Remember we went to school together?"

"Jerry, it's great to see you after all these years . . . And how are things?"

He told me he was running marathons all over the bloody globe, and getting the odd spot of film work between runs. He had just married a twenty-something. This being his third marriage, he hoped it worked out. I told him that I hoped so too!

I needed fresh air, and made my excuses, and fucked off out of there. I ambled back the side road to Friars Walk, but his Banquo-like image haunted me for the night. His sleek black hair, his tall lean frame, his immaculate cut hand-finished suit, his flashy smile. Believe me, this guy made Pierce Brosnan look like an octogenarian – and yet his childhood could be summed up in two words – starvation and deprivation.

Now, he could advertise the food pyramid!

This is what drove me ballistic. Here was Jerry Murphy, the same age as myself, looking as if he just stepped out of a Bond movie. And here was I, who had looked after myself as if I were a prize greyhound, now looking like a battered hedgehog without the hair, and a list of health complaints that could suggest that I could have been the longest serving prisoner in Belsen, or that I had been a compulsive camper in Chernobyl. Believe me when I tell you, that I remember Jerry drinking out of a jam jar, and walking round the streets of Cork in his bare feet in the early sixties.

Nutrition my arse!

It is hard to keep going, in this Valley of Tears, with experiences like that.

But my old life went on, in a kind of a way. The pervasive little bastard, had by now, taken up permanent residency in my big toe, and dissatisfied with that, went on his travels and extended to my upper body in a matter of months. The entire might of the medical fraternity were unable to respond. The medication I was prescribed was totally inadequate, and, despite numerous changes to the medications, and using different combinations, the gout outsmarted the lot. If I told you that a kick in the balls is small fry to the pain of gout, the males out there might have some idea of the pain I was suffering, at this time. On occasions, when my foot would swell up like a roasted tomato, I would have to get injections from my GP, to dampen down the intensity of the pain. I remember on one occasion, it took me two hours to crawl to the bathroom, which was only a matter of yards away from my bedroom, due to the severity of the pain. If this was some retribution by the Gods for sins in my past life, I must have been some bastard when I last roamed the planet. While I perfectly understand that a pain in one's small finger means more to that person than all the suffering of mankind, the pain I'm alluding to is the kind that could easily have you scurrying round the back shed looking for the rope.

Now, every few months was bringing something akin to a new illness into my life, so much so, that I felt in my heart, that my deck was surely crumbling. But, I had a young son, and a patient wife, who by now was sure she had married some kind of human disease freak. My list was endless: gout, high blood pressure, chest pains, liver failure, peptic ulcer, tennis elbow, though I never held a tennis racket in my life. I'm sure my wife must have secretly wished that I would blow up, on one of my many visits to the doctors. With my experience, I hadn't ruled it out either, but I read a motivational book and I became positive. So, I bought another pair of air shoes, a juicer, an exercise bike and I became a vegetarian. But, I wasn't any old vegetarian. No I was a hundred-percenter – truly dedicated to the cause! Whatever else in the line of illness's that might befall me, certainly, mad cow disease would not be found on my chart. I scurried through supermarkets, seeking out vegetarian alternatives. I was so enchanted with Linda McCartney, we might have been lovers. At the very sight of a vegetarian product on the lower shelf, I would fall to my knees faster than any army ranger. I was a man possessed. I knew I had found the Healthy Path – Hatha Yoga.

At last, I arrived at the Golden Gate in my head; all would be well. I would eat and exercise my way back, to be a healthy middle-aged man. Might even have an open shirt and flaunt a medallion. I didn't present such a bad image to the long mirror, if only I lost three stone, and grew a fresh crop of hair. Things were looking up – this bloody book was working. Instead of crawling out of bed, and breakfasting on a cocktail of tablets to get some momentum into my bones, I was looking forward to the challenge that the day threw up. I was juicing like a small enterprise, and collecting nuts and pulses as if I was going to retire to bed for the entire winter. People were remarking that I had a new bounce in my step – I told them that I was shaping up for the marathon.

If only....................

`If only I could get my blood pressure under control, get my liver to function properly, get my chest pains to recede, and above all, to get some relief from the gout, I might make the starting line for the New York marathon.

"Ill weaved ambition how much have thou shrunk."

I was soon on the flat of my back, rosy red toe in the air, tears gathering in my eyes, and the doctor ready with the syringe to ease the fucking pain. My brand new diet had somehow upset my metabolism, and the little bastard took full advantage. Another setback!

"You can only see the stars when the sun goes down."

Well shag that for a yarn.

Four days, on the flat of my back, and my new found dreams gone up in smoke before my very eyes. Somehow the juicer was no longer appealing, the thought of running the New York Marathon seemed as remote as a trip up Mount Everest, but the dog needed walking, so I put on the air shoes again. I was gingerly crawling back into the slow lane once more. The complete trust, of a young smiling son, and the patient support of my wife, helped me up once more – and Linda McCartney was still waiting for me in the aisles of my local supermarket.

So, I still continued on the vegetarian trek.

On my visits to Goleen, in West Cork, I could still look the sheep in the eyes and not feel guilty for having eaten one of their offspring.

Around this time I was acquiring a new title – 'house husband' – that's what the insurance company said I was now. The big world of work, was outside the four walls of the house, while inside, I was trying to find a new place for myself in the world. I looked for God too, but all I found was Tony Quinn, so off I went after him. I followed him to Eccles St., but I didn't find him there, instead, I found a dapper little woman, who recorded my misfortunes, and promised me a better life, when I handed over a few hundred quid. A desperate man with a desperate quest.

To my limited understanding, the whole philosophy behind the Tony Quinn Educo method of success was to quieten the mind through meditation, and thereby, to descend to a deeper level of consciousness where one would then bring up one's special request. And, by totally focusing on that request, would cause the negative aspects surrounding it, to melt away, thereby bringing about success. As a paid-up member, if not a disciple of Tony Quinn, I was entitled to attend a special meeting each Wednesday morning in Eccles Street, where the dapper little woman, gave us a ten minute speech, and the meeting was thrown open to the attending flock. I can tell you that every loser; every cracked up tosser; every religious freak; every hypochondriac in the land; somehow found their way into these meetings. They were worse than myself. At one of these meetings, after a rousing speech about the power of positive thinking, the commanding officer, i.e. the dapper little woman, was asked by one of the attending nutters, if he meditated long and hard enough, would it be possible he could somehow win the Lotto? The dapper little woman was at least consistent, and told him, that if he kept melting away the negatives around his request, you would never know how things might work out. I was growing weary of the melting process, and I melted away myself. I had paid up my full membership fee on joining, but I left my few quid with the dapper little woman, never to return. These quick fixes were not working for me. Meanwhile, back at the medical ranch, things were moving apace, and my team of doctors were discussing the enigma that was me.

One morning, a letter arrived from Trinity College – it was from a medical professor at the college. At first, I thought they were looking for me to donate my body – dead or alive. For my brother always said, that if I ever did donate my body to science research, that they would find a cure for all known human diseases within five years. But it was not that dramatic. After some interchange of letters, between my cardiologist, my nephrologist, my rheumatologist and my G.P., it was suggested that the Professor take a look at me. I duly arrived at the college, and was greeted by the distinguished professor. Following a few sociable exchanges, the affable Professor asked me to firstly name the medication I was taking – here was my opening.

"Emcor, aspirin, cozaar, zyloric, celebrex, zocor, colchicines,"

I rattled them off, as if I was naming the Italian soccer team.

"OK, OK, I get the picture."

He waved his hands nervously around, as if he was conducting the universe.

He knew my type – I would talk medicine with the Pope.

He shone lights into every orifice in my body, gazed down my throat as if he could see my shoelaces, took my blood pressure, got a temperature reading, measured my heartbeat, and belted every moving part in my body with a wooden hammer. Believe me, this man was thorough.

When he had finally finished I stood before him, bare-chested; anxious to hear the verdict."

"Doc, how do I stand?"

He took a long, ponderous moment, to reply.

"Did you ever think you are unlucky?"

He paused, not knowing what to say next.

"You know . . . Being dealt this hand "

My response was quick, and to the point.

"Doc, I have had my days in the sun."

Undaunted, I threw on my shirt and departed the rarefied atmosphere of Trinity College. I had to fight on. Christ I had to fight on.

Luckily, I came from a long line of proud fighting people, and I had inherited their courage. My uncle was one of the fighting men of '16 my great-grandmother once nearly bit off a British army officer's finger, when he endeavoured to remove a note from her mouth, on one of their many raids on her house. My great-grandfather was probably the only one of our clan who had etched his name in history; for he was the man who swore Billy Allen – one of the Manchester Martyr's – into the Fenian movement, in Bandon, County Cork. My great -grandfather, was known as South Gate Jim, and he was the Fenian leader, south of the river, in Cork City, around 1865. On many occasions, O'Donovan Rossa stayed in their house, at Evergreen St., usually disguised as a woman, while on the run from the British forces.

So, it was no great surprise, with so much of their blood coursing through my veins, that I choose the military path myself, when I was young. So, in the early '60's when I was just a slip of a lad, I joined the local FCA unit, in Cork. Well, to be more precise, I was more an athletic volunteer than a soldier – this is why I was never fitted out for a uniform. Simple things like uniforms could wait – I was now a member of the 23rd Battalion FCA – and available for selection on the athletic team.

It is important to understand the mind-set that permeated the defence forces, around this time. As the country was comparatively peaceful, except for the outrages of a few Teddy Boys on a Saturday night; the 'big brass' were always looking out for something to entertain the uniformed boys in green. The North of Ireland, at this stage, was as quiet as a monastic settlement, so the 'big brass' in the army, turned their attention to competition on the athletic track.

And this is where I came in.

During our summer holidays from school, we travelled to special military athletic competitions, all over the country. I was easily spotted in the back of the truck; I was the soldier with the Fair Isle jumper. It is hard at this remove now, to have any clear idea, as to why I was not decked out in a uniform. But, I got my few bob every Thursday, along with my dinner and a mug of senna and I was as happy as a pig in shit. Whatever the army was doing for me, I was improving my sprinting like a well-bred two-year old. I ran round Ballincollig, Fermoy, Phoenix Park and The Curragh like a scalded cat winning all before me. I was the star performer, wherever I went: 100 yards, 220 yards, 440 yards, long jump. With my assembled collection of trophies, I was responsible for an extra shift at Waterford Glass. At presentations, before the assembled 'hob knobs', it would always be made clear, by the ever-vigilant quartermaster in charge of our unit, that a new uniform was just about ready for me.

But who worried about trivia like that, in light of such an outstanding talent.

They were glad to have me inside or outside a uniform. About this time, word was passed down to me, through the grapevine, that, perhaps I was destined for greater things in the military arena, and that someday in the future I might make a good Officer. But, it was pointed out to me, that this would require a tricky piece of footwork, in order to make it into the Cadets. The intake into the Army Cadetship, at this time, was very low – perhaps something in the region of only twenty males – and every ruse known to mankind was used to secure a place. Someone up there wanted me as an Officer, so therefore, the Sergeant of our Unit was detailed to mark my card. Having the profile of being an inter-county player with Cork was no burden, and my reputation as a track runner was spreading like an Australian bushfire. Although I was no Einstein in the classroom, my Leaving Cert results were good enough to get me over any examination hurdle, and with a fine pair of hobnail boots, and a heavy pair of woollen socks, I could reach up to the height requirements. Therefore, I was a serious contender for cadetship, with a few supporters on the wings. So, in the heel of the hunt, I was fitted out in that illusive uniform, and ordered to turn up for Basic Training at Spike Island.

My mother and sisters were all-a-dither, when I paraded before them, in my splendid uniform in the kitchen. I marched to-and-fro, as my boots beat an everlasting tattoo, on the kitchen tiles. Unbiased, they all agreed that I had the makings of a fine Officer, and that the Army were the real winners here. I had to remind them, that I was still only a Private, of the lowest order in the FCA – but they would have none of it, wanting to believe, that one of their own was a hero-in-the-making. When they had photographed me from every angle in the kitchen, and when the neighbours had a gawk at me, I was released from duty. My God, I was so tired from all the parading, that I could have come straight from The Congo.

Whatever ambition I had, to join the Army as an Officer, vanished completely during that first week of training on Spike Island. A few, jumped-up, two-star, neck-shaven Corporals, were conducting the course. We are talking the lowest form of human life here. Scumbags, who ranted and raved, fucked and blinded everyone in sight from dawn-to-dusk. These guys hadn't chips on their shoulders – they had concrete blocks. Through bullying, threatening, and subjecting all-and-sundry to brutality, they got their way.

Did I hate these bastards?

If I had been anywhere near a loaded gun, I would have been severely tempted, to give each and every one of them, a present in the back of their skulls.

Jumped-up boozy boys.

"Clionaig airm"

Clionaig your own fucking airm.

I knew now, for sure, that an army life was not for me. If I had to put up with this shit for two years, while training, God alone knows how I would end up.

When my two weeks basic training was up, I left behind Spike Island, promising never to return again. I hated everything about the Army – so now I stayed away from all things military, and never reported to my FCA Unit, in Cork City. Like most people in the '60's, we did not have a 'phone at home, so therefore, I was out of humanities reach.

One afternoon, as I was doing some job applications, I heard an almighty scream, coming from the front room. I thought at first, that the mother was getting a bad turn and was calling out for help, so I rushed in. She was gesticulating in the direction of the window.

"Jesus, the Army are here to arrest you. You never returned your uniform. Look the truck is outside . . ."

Sure enough the FCA truck was outside with my old Sergeant at the helm. I opened the door, but before I could speak, the Sergeant had the window down in the truck.

"All set for the Curragh Sports Meeting this evening? Hurry up, for Christ sake."

I grabbed my gear and spikes.

It was okay from now on – all the Army wanted was a runner and not a Soldier. I joined the other lads in the back of the truck, explained my absence to them, amid many jibes, as we sped towards the Curragh.

When the truck stopped at some midland town, we were all directed towards this roadside café. The hungry lads sped down the long entrance towards the tables, and as soon as the waitress caught sight of the uniforms, she shouted in the direction of the kitchen.

"Is the black pudding ready for the FCA?"

The outburst of laughter from the other customers nearly shattered the glass roof.

Now how would an Officer-in-waiting deal with all that? I deserted the main body and sloped over to the corner. There are times in this life, when a fairisle jumper is your only man. When the black pudding was sunk and the tea drunk, we made our way once more to the army truck – these athletes did not need any special feeding or any molly-coddling – and soon we were on our way to further fame and fortune. At the sports meeting we won all before us; to such an extent, that at one presentation, I overheard a Senior Army Officer utter, that he wished that we would shag off, and leave some trophies for the rest of the competitors. The sound of singing, emanating from the back of an army truck, on the Dublin to Cork road, must have sounded strange to the onlookers on that night. We were so delighted; we could have been a bunch of soldiers triumphantly returning from a war. But that glorious day, marked the end of my participation in all things military, and I said a sad farewell and hung up my fairisle jumper for good, as I moved on to pastures new.

CHAPTER TWO

Thinking back and reflecting on those far-off mad days, it is difficult to get a handle or to even remember on how we perceived the world at that time. The world of an eighteen year old is a totally different place to that of a forty-five year-old man.

No outsider in the world will ever have any inkling what is going on inside the four walls of a house. In my own situation, for most of the time I was going about doing a few chores and trying to figure out as Peggy Lee sang –

"Is this all there is to life."

I was writing the odd short story and composing the occasional poem but nothing on a consistent basis. My life was lived between doctors' appointments, and it seemed that even between those appointments I was supplying blood by the bucket-load for analyses. Being on a medical merry-go-round and spinning nowhere, I hated the mornings most of all, because on waking I felt as if I had been through twelve rounds with 'Iron Mike.'

After many years of lousy health I was still presenting a visage to the world as if things were pretty normal. Instead of trying to figure out the answer to the Theory of Theories or perhaps delving deeper into the Second Law of Thermodynamics in order to keep the old grey matter in some kind of working order, I'm afraid to admit that the only analysis I was undertaking was on the sports pages of The Daily Mirror. I was still knocking some use out of the air shoes but my speed of walking was slowing to octogenarian pace, which led to a very embarrassing situation one morning on my gallops when a man passed me out on crutches. I sighed for those faraway days when I could take on a greyhound on a straight hundred.

"Oh, how the mighty have fallen".

I was investigating ways of trying to improve my walking speed; thereby improving my fitness, and hoping to have the benefits filter into other aspects of my life.

My usual practice was to weigh myself each morning and record it in a diary – no problem on that score – a steady fifteen stone – no change for yonks. One Saturday morning my wife arrived home from a shopping expedition with a present under her oxter; a special forty-fifth birthday gift for me. I quickly unwrapped it to reveal something I had desired for ages – digital weighing scales. Without further ado I hopped up. Christ I nearly blew a gasket!

Seventeen stone two pounds – ah, something wrong with that scales.

Sure wasn't I fifteen stone for the last four years; the bloody thing must be giving false readings. My wife proceeded to read the accompanying leaflet:

"This machine is always accurate to point two of a pound"

I hopped up on the scales again. Same result.

I jumped up on the old scales.

Fifteen stone it lied.

I grabbed the dog and weighed him with me.

Fifteen stone.

Everything in the fucking world weighed fifteen stone according to the old scales.

In desperation I managed to pull my wife onto the scales with me, we were perched on the scales Torvil and Dean-like with my wife's leg shooting out before her.

Again it didn't deviate – fifteen stone exactly.

Jesus I'm in the super category league and I didn't even know it – no wonder the guy with the crutches passed me out in the park.

I was distraught. I could have lambasted my wife for buying the scales but I simmered down in a few minutes.

"Do you know something, it's those shaggin' tablets, those blood pressure tablets are worse than any growth hormones".

I related the story I heard about a woman in Crumlin who put on so much weight from blood pressure tablets that one night she fell through the bed.

"Throw a handful of those bloody tablets into the cattle in the morning and they'd be no need to put them out on grass".

I was demented for days. Each time I would pass the long mirror in the hallway I'd stop and have a gawk. I was growing bigger by the day. The world was witnessing the birth of another Sumo wrestler before its very eyes. Now that I was aware of my true weight I felt helpless to respond; in desperation I turned to the Internet.

Diets I looked for and by Christ diets I got – everything from the cabbage water diet to the F plan to the Atkins diet. How on earth was there anyone overweight at all?

Being a coward I selected what I considered the easiest plan and obviously the less intrusive. Though I couldn't have my bread and eat it, I could have my sausage and eat it if I chose the Atkins. There was just one tiny consideration – I was a vegetarian. So cabbage water won out. From imbibing the first mug of cabbage water on the Friday morning to the first weigh-in on the Monday I had lost seven pounds. To say I was ecstatic was the understatement of the year.

No matter how shaggin awful it tasted I was going to stick with this now .....

It worked ..... it worked ....

I was already contemplating the new me. If I could lose weight at this rate Christ I'd be able to ride the Epsom Derby by June. In an effort not to run away with myself I settled for a weight loss of five stone – this would have me hovering on the twelve stone mark – perfectly acceptable for a man of my stature. I spent the whole week skulling cabbage water and I was so enthused that the galling taste was almost acceptable. By Friday I could not leave the bed as I was unable to get trousers to stay on me. God only knew what I had lost in the week. Although I was scheduled for a Monday morning weigh-in I could not resist the temptation to hop on the scales; I had to look again. I was a good smidgeon under the sixteen stone. I had lost the best part of sixteen pounds. My wife hopscotched it to Dunnes Stores to secure a smaller trouser so I could arise and tell the world the wonderful news. There is something magical about achievement – something that lifts the spirit and portrays to the wider world that man can achieve when body and mind is focussed one hundred per cent. I was a new man growing thinner by the day.

But as usual my wife intervened and endeavoured to quell my dieting crusade.

She had been down that road on many occasions before, and understood very well my nature and how I was prone to get carried away with the project on hand.

She knew full well how many escapades had ended in heartache if not disaster.

With my underlying serious health problems she knew very well that I was very restricted in what I could and couldn't do. I was a totally different animal.

If a felt reasonably well two days in a row I would start planning something which would never in a million years become a reality. I was a dreamer and a bit of a poet, and this stemmed from my childhood in Cork.

When I was a very young boy I spent hours listening to my grandmother reciting poetry. She was one of the most remarkable people that I ever encountered. Her incredible memory for stories and verse was legendry. Although well into her nineties, she could recall stories of her childhood with amazing clarity. Her father was involved in an attack on Ballyknocken Barracks way back during the Fenian rising of 1867; he was arrested some days later, and subsequently brought to trial in the courthouse in Cork. My grandmother learned by heart every word spoken in the trial by both the Judge and her father, and was able to recall them word-perfect up to the day of her death. I learned songs, stories and poems from her sitting around her fireside; and I loved every minute of it. Once when asked to sing a song at some family get-together – and me not ten years at the time – started off much to the amazement of the gathering :

"Please let me like a soldier fall, upon some open plain"

I was performing opera if you don't mind – a little number from Maritana by William Wallace.

I don't ever remember being asked to sing again.

My grandmother was the perfect tutor, and she possessed the greatest ingredient for that job – enthusiasm. Yeats once said that education was not just about imparting knowledge but lighting a fire; in that respect my grandmother had it one hundred per cent right. I carried that fire, sometimes a flame, and more times just a smouldering idea with me through life.

As with my grandmother my grandfather also lived to the great old age of ninety-five. It seemed to a young pair of eyes that this was all they had in common.

My grandfather hailed from a Protestant family and had a totally different outlook regarding the Irish struggle. He had not the fire and brimstone that my grandmother possessed, he regarded life as something to be enjoyed, and his actions reflected that philosophy on a daily basis. It was no great wonder then that his pipe and his birds were the most important things in his life.

And it was from my grandfather I picked up the practical experience. At his side I learned how to cut and prepare plug tobacco and bit by bit learned the art of filling his pipe using the correct pressure. As the whole ritual took an age a young boy had to learn to be patient. I waited by his side for him to light up the pipe and send smoke curling to the ceiling. He asked me to name all the animals I saw in the smoke, and I strained and strained my neck until the last piece of smoky cloud disappeared and I had named all my animals that sped towards the ceiling. When all the animals had faded the aroma of the smoke hung in the air and like incense in the church changed the atmosphere to a more peaceful setting. After breakfast, lighting up the pipe was always the first act of the day. Then when the pipe smoking was over we would go up the winding stairs to the first landing. Here he would pause for breath, before beginning the journey to the next level of the house where the bird room was situated. At the sound of the creaking door opening my heart would rise in my chest with anticipation of feeding the birds. My grandfather was known in those days in Cork as a bird fancier.

All the birds in the room were wild birds that my grandfather had caught and caged in the Lee Fields. When the work of feeding, cleaning and watering was complete it was time for the second smoke of the day and the whole slow ritual commenced again. Who cared about time – we had all the time in the world. When I attended school on my first day my grandfather walked all the way to the school with sandwiches for my ten o clock break, and waited outside the old school gate for me to appear. I was never more excited in my life than when I saw him there.

"I just dropped over these few sandwiches to you; I knew you would be hungry by now."

He peered in from outside the closed gate as I dug into the fresh bread, and when the bell rang I had to return to my class and leave him all alone at the gate. And he did make that trip many times, and for me it was the most welcome sight in the world.

But tempus fugit and soon I was attending secondary school, but I still maintained the close relationship with him. He took ill and was removed to hospital and when my mother and myself would visit him the one question on his lips would be:

"Did you bring my clothes?"

It became his mantra.

After a dozen or so heart attacks, and as many fears that he would die within hours, my mother decided to bring him home to our house. Against all the odds he lived almost a year before he eventually died. Many years later I wrote this poem in his honour.

REMEMBERING.

Vivid
That white paper lunch bag
Held in brown tobacco fingers
Vivid those hands
Craftsman's hands, old, mahogany stained
Eyes: grandfather eyes
Seeking me out
Through a rusty schoolyard gate

Later
That long walk to Lee Fields
Where we picked piss-a-beds
For his unsuspecting birds
Goldfinches and brown linnets
Our riverbank shadows
Criss-crossing, mingling
Under a low September sky
Gathering together
Bunches of wormy weeds,
Slimy stems with weepy yellow heads
Our golden harvest

Vivid also
Little whitewashed bird room
The chirping birds
The scattered seed
The half assembled cages
The chaos
With the smell and taste of freedom

Dusty skylight
Through which a tiny eye
Could see another Heaven
Years later
When illness struck
I stood at the foot of the bed
Understood when he waved me away
Those other souls were seeking his company
AT Curraghkippane
Nestling between wood and river
I said farewell
And as I left the graveyard
His wild songbirds were gathering
Hovering above
Little feathered Angels
Ready to carry him
Across a brightening sky
So that his brown fingers
His mahogany hands
Could touch another gate
Another Paradise

CHAPTER THREE

The first night I landed in St. Lazarre station in Paris I could feel the excitement rising in my veins. I had just arrived there from the Republic of Cork; with my French phrase book at the ready. To say that I did not have any knowledge of the French language would be incorrect – I knew less than that. In order to gather my thoughts and plan my next move, I pulled up a high chair in the station's long bar, and when approached by the bar lady I pointed in the direction of the beer.

The bar lady shouted something like 'grow' of 'grose' in my direction, I indicated with an exaggerated gesture of my hands that I wanted the biggest drink available in Paris. From her smile I knew she thought that another 'one' had strayed into the web. But I was in Paris at long last fighting fit, brim full of energy, twenty-six years old and foot lose and fancy free. The seven wonderful years I spent at the Ford Motor Company were now behind me and new horizons beckoned. As soon as I had gulped down the drink, I opened my palms to the bar lady and she gratefully grabbed a fistful of money – she was still beaming as I left the station.

Paris exploded in my face – the noise of the traffic, the buzz of the people as they sped right left and centre, the lights flashing their messages to the heaving masses, the wonderful aromas escaping from the cafes – yes I was in Paris and it was the one spot on the planet that I wanted to be at this time in my life. It sent the adrenalin coasting around my body like a jet stream out of control.

Movement is life say the Bolshoi Ballet ... I'll drink to that!

I grabbed the first taxi in the line – I was surprised it was a lady driver – the first time in my life I had encountered a female taxi driver. When I had settled into the back of the cab, I called out to her

"Hotel' .....   'Cheap'...... 'Cheap'

She took off like a scalded cat, totally ignoring me. I was thinking how brave this woman was – and her in Paris – when suddenly this monstrosity of a head peeped over the back seat and peered straight into my eyes as I turned to investigate.

A big black rottweiler was eyeing me up.

"Well, she has to be paid anyway, I thought to myself, no chance of doing a runner here."

I'm pretty sure she took me round the same block three or four times, but eventually she stopped, pointed to the door opposite, asked for money, the dog growled and I put a ten spot into her sweaty little palm.

"Buy a bone for the dog with the change."

I uttered bravely from the security of the footpath.

"Oh thank you very much Monsieur."

She replied much to my surprise.

I approached the big heavy door and with a fair bit of apprehension rang the bell. Soon I heard the footsteps and the sound of a large heavy bolt being drawn at the door. It opened. I forgot what I was about to say, but the man, seeing my case waved me in and beckoned me to follow him to the desk. He was a chubby man, with swarthy features, and he pushed a pen in my direction uttering something in French at the same time.

"Do you speak English?" I blurted out.

"Yes, Yes, English is spoke here."

I booked in for three nights, surrendered my passport, paid my money and found out that they had no bar, no food and no stairs. But they did have a musty smell that hung in the air like a motionless cloud. Christ this is some 'hotel' I thought to myself but it is cheap.

"Stairs fall in two days ago, use the lift, take use of the lift," said the swarthy man now smiling. The lift rattled its way up the third floor and I emerged to half yellow light and that same choking smell. This floor appeared grubbier than the reception, but I was not in this hotel to allocate any stars; all I needed was somewhere to put my head for a few nights until I got my bearings.

It was the five-o-clock train that woke me – I looked out the window and there before my eyes was St.Lazarre Station. The whore in the taxi did bring me around the block; no wonder she needed the protection of a Rottweiler. My throat was as dry as the Gobi desert, so up I got at that unearthly hour, found the dodgy lift and let myself out into the Paris air. The narrow street was teeming girls – all ages, all sizes, and all colours, with skirts just below their tonsils. The penny dropped at last!

I was stuck right in the heart of the red light district. I moved along the narrow street which was devoid of any traffic. As I ambled curiously along the footpath some girls approached me in a manner that suggested that they weren't looking for my autograph. They reeked of cheap perfume which was only slightly better smelling than the aromas available at my 'hotel'. At the corner, just opposite the station, I read the name of the street – Rue Amsterdam.

What a place to pitch my tent.

I was lucky that my mother wasn't visiting me for the weekend.

Though it was early morning the city was buzzing; the sun was now beginning to throw its natural light on the streets and the café owners were rattling tables and chairs as they set up for another day on Boulevard Haussmann.

As I drank my coffee I thought how quiet Pana was right now – the road sweepers in Cork were hardly out yet – and yet Paris was moving into full swing, and I was dizzy adjusting to the whole pace of things. But I was up for the challenges that this great city would throw at me.

Three nights I had planned, but three weeks later I was still in the 'Hilton without the Stairs'. But it was cheap – doss house cheap. From my comings and goings it appeared to me that I was the only bone fide resident in the 'hotel'. The ladies of the street used the 'hotel' day and night as a sort of meeting parlour. They gathered towels from the swarthy guy in reception – who appeared to me to be on duty day and night – as they accompanied their prey up the dodgy lift. From the number of towels the girls collected over the day, I guess they had to be the cleanest women in all of Paris. The girls also got used to me coming and going, and they now adopted a different posture – smiling rather than propositioning – when I would pass them on the street. Like the fire brigade they were on call twenty-four hours a day, and I suppose like the fire brigade, they were doing a similar job in the sense that they also were putting out fires albeit different types of fires.

As I went about Paris I had my head stuck in the phrase book day and night.

'Oui' and 'Non' did not present too much of a problem, but anything other than that and I was out of my depth. The perceived wisdom of the generation was to find a French girlfriend who did not speak English and, by my sheer endeavour to communicate with her, I'd be speaking French like a true Parisian in a matter of weeks.

But it was a catch twenty-two situation.

Every Mademoiselle that happened to cross my path had better English than me, so there was no point in wooing those particular females; they had no function in my conniving plan. And I had more pressing hygiene factors – the cash was disappearing at a rate of knots – so some action was called for on the employment front in order to keep hunger if not starvation at bay.

Funerals in Paris were expensive items.

As procrastination is the art of keeping up with yesterday I decided to move – look to the future and hatch my plan. Monday was dedicated action day – I would not return to the 'Hilton' without a job under my belt. I set about the task with great gusto, determined to be on some buggers payroll before the day darkened. My first port of call was a recruitment agency.

Bingo! The company up the road were looking for a general worker.

When I showed the girl in the agency my international driver's license her eyes lit up. Believe me if I showed a Ph.D. from Oxford she couldn't have got more excited. With my little card from the agency firmly grasped in my hand I hot-footed it up to my prospective employer. I couldn't make arse or tail of the company signs over the door and my nerves at this stage were coming to the boil; but hunger is a great motivator. I gathered the courage if not the madness and went inside and flashed my card, as swift as any FBI agent, in the direction of the receptionist. Without further ado, and with very little pleasantries, she ushered me to the inner sanctum where a secretary was hammering on a typewriter as if she was possessed by some demented spirit. The secretary came to an abrupt halt, peered in my direction and took command of the proceedings.

"English, you are English?"

"No, Irish," I said.

"Great, great, I love the Irish."

I was reassured.

She seemed glad of the opportunity to practice her English and she proceeded to tell me about the job vacancy. She scribbled a few details about me; handed them to the Big Chief when he appeared, and retreated once more behind her typewriter from whence she came. The Fear Mór shook my hand, offered me a seat, looked at my details and proceeded with his soliloquy. I hadn't a bull's notion what he was saying, but every time he would look in my direction I would smile and bow my head. He went on and on, now employing his hands and waving them as if he was conducting the Boston Pops Orchestra. My eyes and ears were glued to him, hoping that in some way I might understand a word or two – but to no avail. I could feel the eyes of the secretary on me, and the tension had now taken full control of my body, from my shoelaces to the top of my head. I was absolutely terrified that any second he would spring a question and throw it in my direction. But I was lucky – this guy was too much in love with his own voice. As he rabbited on I threw a few 'Qui's' and 'Non's' in his direction whenever it seemed appropriate. Eventually he came to a stop, stood up, and once more stretched out his hand in my direction and disappeared into a back office. The secretary ushered me to the front door laughing all the way, she was well aware that I had not the bulls what the man said.

"You won't believe this; you are starting here on Monday morning, better brush up on your French in the meantime."

Monday morning came, and if I had a handful of Roche 15. I would have popped them without any hesitation. I left the "Hilton" about seven-o-clock full of trepidation, and as I weaved my way past the 'Girls' out on Rue Amsterdam, I resisted the temptation to turn back and give the job a skip. The thought of starving on the streets of Paris was too strong and I kept going. Everything was flying about in my head – what will happen when the Big Chief will find out that I haven't a word of French – he'll probably kick me out on my arse or maybe he'll call the cops for me making such a prick of him. I was not carrying a rational head on my shoulders. As I approached the company's door I saw this guy – complete with bulldog eyes – running in my direction and frantically tapping the face of his watch and shouting at me.

"Veet…. Veet'

"Camio…..camio'

He pointed to a small lorry parked across the road, and this out of control geezer whom I had never laid eyes on before, almost pushed me across the road in front of him. He pointed to the driver's seat – Christ he wants me to drive the fucking thing – I had never driven anything bigger than an escort in my life. If I was fearful two minutes before, I was shitting myself now. I did as I was instructed and took the seat behind the wheel. The moustached little fucker beside me in the passenger's seat was complaining about me being late, he was employing the same tapping antics on his watch as the bulldog-eyes man. The lorry had an unusual design, insofar, as the three guys in the back were able to push their heads over the division and look into the cab. They too were complaining like fuck.

"Allez, allez", shouted Mustachio.

The chorus in the back took up the chant.

The lorry felt awkward – everything was on the wrong side. But I got it started and away I went into the Paris traffic. If I wanted a fistful of Roche previous to this, a bucket of them was required now. The crew were shouting out the instructions.

"A gauche, ici," – I would turn left.

"A droit, ici," – I would turn right.

"Tout droit," – straight ahead.

The traffic was skimming me left and right and the heat was building inside me to Sahara temperatures. The sweat was flowing freely down my back as I was headed in the direction of the Arc de Triomphe, with the passengers still roaring out their manic instructions. I was now in one of the lanes circumnavigating the Arc with lanes of traffic to my left and to my right, traffic in front of me and behind me, and the bastards were still shouting like frenzied wild animals. Twice they brought me round the Arc – just for the fun of it. Cars were whizzing left, right and centre and sounding their horns at me and the boys in the back were now breaking their bollucks's laughing at me.

That did it.

I stopped the lorry on the spot – halfway round The Arc – grabbed a wheel brace that was lying next to me in the cab and, with five generations of Archer madness, launched my counter attack.

"The next bastard who opens his mouth will find his fucking head out on the road," I was now screaming and waving the wheel brace in the air like a lunatic. They understood that in any language.

They were shocked into absolute silence. After some moments elapsed, and when the lorry was as a quiet as the Curraghkippane cemetery, there was a tap on the window of the lorry. I gave the motorcycle cop the OK sign and proceeded on my way. My crew in the lorry had encountered a raging Irishman and they were still recovering from the experience.

'Mustachio' – being a kind of charge-hand now gave the instructions.

As we moved out past the Bois de Boulogne, I wondered what in the wide world had I let myself in for – and this only my first day on duty.

On returning to work the following day it was evident that news of the attempted murder of the crew had filtered back to base. As I walked through the back office, the faces of the office workers lit up as I came into focus.

'Bulldog' – my new boss – was waiting for me, bulging eyes ready to pop out on the ground at any time.

"Monsieur Jim, I now know that you speak no French, and you try kill workman yesterday. What we do now with you?"

I stood there with the blankest expression I could muster.

He gave a hint of a grin.

"We see, look we see, work for week anyhow."

"Go to camio now they are waiting for you."

"Merci Monsieur," I replied, taking him by complete surprise and made my way to the infamous camio. I knew in my water that Bulldog was my kind of man.

Once more, the secretary who had been viewing proceedings from afar followed me on to the street.

"Look Jim, they have to keep you here otherwise they will have no driver for the lorry, the other drivers are all suspended from driving by the law. The company cannot get any qualified drivers in Paris."

I thanked her for the vital information.

She smiled a gorgeous smile, and I thought to myself as I approached the camio, that I might be practising more than English with this lady in the future.

'Mousathcio' and his loyal band were already in situ.

"Travail … Tres important … Aujourd'hui … Compris."

'Mustachio', was speaking slowly and directly into my face as if his batteries were running down. I nodded, and the second day driving in hell was about to begin.

After an hours driving – ducking and diving through the traffic – and listening to boring instructions from the mono-toned 'Moustachio', we arrived at our destination. Two monstrous gates were flung open, and the security guards waved me into position at the steps of the building. Once inside another posse of security guards met us, and soon we were loading the steel boxes onto the camio. The crew got going, and in less than an hour, we had the canvass overcoat firmly fixed over our cargo and ready to roll. Two police cars came speeding through the gates, and prepared to take up positions at the front and rear of the camio. With yours truly at the helm, 'Mustachio', my guiding light by my side, the police cars now positioned at front and rear of us, we rolled out the gates. But there were more surprises in store – we were joined by four motorbike police outriders who took up positions left and right of us. On we sped through the traffic, 'Moustachio' spitting out the instructions to me, the crew fast asleep in the back of the camio along with the priceless collection of books from the national Library, and a posse of police accompanying us on our way. Finally we reached our destination, another set of gates opened up for us and we bade farewell to our illustrious bodyguards. When we had despatched our cargo, we headed into the mayhem of traffic once more, our hour of fame well and truly over.

Life went on with the crew and me but I was never accepted as one of them. They would occasionally try to put one over on me – the trick was to order drink for the group – they would plan between themselves to drink it as fast as possible and to skedaddle out of the café without me noticing them, thereby leaving me to pick up the tab. But I quickly wised up. And I got more than my own back when they were seated at one of our watering holes, I ordered doublers for the lot and scurried out the back door and hid myself away in the camio and waited for the reaction. Though they were furious they never let on, especially as I was positioned once more beside the wheel brace. It was becoming a true friend. From dealing on a daily basis with the low life on Paris – my workmates – I was also picking up the odd bit of argot, and my nose was never too far away from the phrase book. I had already enrolled at Alliance Francaise in Boulevard Raspail and attending classes five nights a week. With the constant few francs in my pocket, I decided to leave the swarthy man and his towels, the Hilton without the stairs, and the girls of Rue Amsterdam, and took myself up street, if not upmarket, to a bedsit in Montmartre. 'Bulldog Eyes' was showing more confidence in me day-by-day, so much so, that he gave me a big bonus at the end of the month, and I took the secretary to practice her English over the biggest Couscous Royal in all of Paris. I held her hand after the meal, but it was as cold as a dead mackerel, and the smile had gone from her face. She felt tired and left to catch the Metro home. I stayed on, drank another few glasses with the Algerian waiter with the broken English, spoke about the student riots, and resolved the Northern Ireland problem, before catching a cab to Montmartre.

I loved this part of Paris – it had everything. We had the painters and artists in Montmarte, up the hill nearer to heaven we had the Basilica Sacre Coeur, while appropriately enough down the steps in Pigalle we had the sex shops and prostitutes – a lively cocktail for any twenty something to behold. I spent hours, particularly at weekends, listening to the haunting music of the nuns at the Basilica. Their stillness, serenity, and the mesmeric sounds almost suggested that they were touching heaven itself. Whatever magic they possessed it always got me deep in the pit of my stomach, and when I emerged into the light of day from the Basilica I almost floated down those famous steps.

Once in Paris, I wanted to explore – to go to the highways and byways and feel the pulse of that city.   Saturday was dedicated exploration day. I would rise at seven, do my hours training, take a shower and was then set up for the day. The plan was simple – just take off in the metro, change metros and trains randomly, and in this way I would often dispatch myself to some pocket of the city unseen by the tourist's eye.   If there was anything of interest ranging from a flea market to racing frogs I would be nosing about. Sometimes the exercise proved fruitless, and the best thing on show was a ten-storey block of flats. I would simply repeat the exercise, get myself underground again, and hopefully emerge in a more interesting place. On one such occasion I found myself back at St Lazarre Station, and I took the opportunity to see if the bar lady who had taken my fist of money was still in residence and whether was she still smiling from my first encounter with her. But it appeared she was gone from the scene – at least for that day anyway. I ordered a large pot of tea, cocked my nose in the air to take in the garlic smell that wafted through the air and listened to the trains and metros bellowing at each other in the background.

It was nice to watch the world roll by!

Suddenly I was conscious of someone behind me. I swung my stool around from the counter and before me stood the biggest man I had ever seen in my life, dressed in full army uniform complete with de Gaulle – Style cap. His twinkling eyes smiled down on me from on high.

"Dutch? English?"

"No … Irish," I replied.

"Oh brilliant, great … do you mind if I join you?"

"Be my guest," I was delighted with the company.

"You're the first Irishman I have ever seen drinking tea in a bar … here let me buy you a drink …. My name is Jonny Merkens."

"Jim Archer, and I only drink tea when the moon is asleep."

"Make an exception for one day, try a whiskey"

"Oh go on, I'll be sociable …just for the day that's in it."

"Madame, deux Whiskey Irlandaise, sil vous plait."

The drinks secured, he wasted no time in getting down to business. He told me he was the recruitment officer for the Legion Estranger – The French Foreign to you and me. He went on to explain that he operated all over France recruiting for that august body, and that he himself was Dutch, had been in three armies – Dutch, American and The French Foreign Legion and that he spoke thirteen languages. I knew what was coming down the line.

He lifted the glass to his mouth and finished his drink with the one swig, and before I could utter a word he had another pair of drinks ordered.

"Would you hold onto your cap here Jonny, this stuff will blow my head off."

But he ignored me and re-arranged the new drinks in front of us.

"Now that you know everything about me, tell me something about yourself."

"Everything," I said.

"Well, the important bits anyway."

The first belt of the whiskey had already hit the spot, and that warmness was spreading through my body, and the whole world was taking on a grand mellow feeling. Behind us St. Lazarre station was filling to capacity, and the lunatic manning the tannoy system was working himself into a frenzy blaring out times and destinations – it's a wonder the roof stayed on.

It was impossible to hear never mind conduct a conversation and The Big Man spoke:

"Let's get out of here, and find some place, somewhere quieter."

We both finished the whiskey; he threw half-a-weeks wages to the bar lady for the drink, and we were soon winding our merry way through the streets of Paris. I felt liberated – Monsieur Moneybags had a small bank in his pocket. He hailed a taxi and we headed for our next port of call, which was a café near Boulevard St.Michel. Here we had aperitifs, and lunch and wine; and calvados, and more calvados; and I told him my life story, and how I came to Paris to study French and to be a Bohemian for a while, and to run like a lunatic through the Bois de Boulogne, and that someday I might go to the Sorbonne and be another famous Irishman in Paris. He told me I was great material for the French Foreign Legion, and that if ever I wanted to join, all I had to do was to take myself to Rue du Moulinet in Rouen and they would be delighted to enrol me any time.

And fill up my pockets with many francs.

Of course they would send me to Marseilles for six months for French lessons and training before I hit the Dark Continent.

"Look," I said, "put me down as a good prospect."

The drink was already talking.

We celebrated that with the best bottle of champagne the house could offer. We were lucky that we could hold our drink – I was young and fit, he was as tall as an oak tree, so a couple of stiff black espressos brought us back from the brink, but only to resume in another watering hole a few hours later near the Trocadero. More food and wine, more French government francs, and two soul-mates now incoherent in any of thirteen languages. Over the day, I found that this man was interested in everything from horse racing to military history, and everything else that was going on in the universe and beyond. He had a particular interest in the Irish Writers and was very well acquainted with W.B. Yeats. When we spoke about Yeats; me, now fortified by a day's drinking, stood up on my chair and recited to the assembled multitude:

"The Song of the Wondering Aengus"
And when I came to the last verse:
Though I am old with wondering
Through hollow lands and hilly lands,
I will find out where she is gone,
And kiss her lips and take her hands;
And walk among long dappled grass,
And pluck 'til time and times are done
The silver apples of the moon,
The golden apples of the sun.

The entire crowd cheered.

Christ, if I had recited the poem in French, the crowd would have pulled the house down; but it proved once more that spontaneity was alive and well and living in that fantastic city. Jonny too was bowled over by the impromptu performance, and this was his final confirmation that I was poor material for The French Foreign Legion.

"You'd be wasted with our lot, stick with the poetry."

He was no mug. I was never military material.

A quick sup for the road, and Jonny was hailing a taxi, stuffing a wad of notes into the driver's hand, bidding me farewell and I was leaving his company and The French Foreign Legion forever. I had a head like a rotten turnip the next day, but it was eased when I remembered that it was not my money that was chucked over the counter. Viva La France.

Attending Alliance Francaise gave me a gateway to the world; every student in my particular class came from a different country, and it made for great fun during language laboratory classes. Repeating the French sounds made for very interesting contrasts; for example, my sing-song Cork tones mixed with the dull Russian accent sounded like an oboe on the piss. We had a female teacher who moved around the lab in constant hysterics, listening to the various sounds emanating from the booths. The Chinese and Japanese sounded like demented birds inside an Avery, while the British and Americans did not seem to mind what sounds they were emitting, as long as their voices were heard over the rest. As each week drew on, we became a very close group of people; we could have come from the same parish in Ireland rather than from the four corners of the earth. At this stage I was attending classes in the evening time – I severely needed the few francs to keep body and soul together so I had to continue to work. After class, a bunch of us would retreat to the local watering hole, after eating our subsidised meal with the compliments of the French Government. Within our group, was a beautiful demure girl, whose father was Dutch and mother Chinese, and she spoke the most wonderful and colourful English. Being a shrewdie from Cork I detected that she had more than a passing interest in yours truly, and while pretending to brush up on her English – her English by the way was better than my own – was patiently wooing me into her web. One evening the door in the classroom opened, and in walked our new student, and what a student she was; the most exotic creature I ever laid eyes on. She was beautiful beyond description. Our tutor took great pleasure in telling us that she once won "The Miss Jamaica" title and was a finalist in the "Miss Universe". No one was surprised.

Guess who won the jackpot.

Moi.

Catlike, she moved towards me, and sat down beside me at the next desk; I didn't murmur a word of protest as she smiled in my direction and stretched out those long legs. Education was definitely paying off for me. My Chinese friend didn't look too pleased – Christ, I thought this could be the makings of me – two fantastic creatures could be going into battle for my affections and I haven't lifted a finger.

I thought about the pub afterwards; all thoughts of learning French verbs dissipated in the Parisian evening. Miss Jamaica and I got on like a house on fire. When she discovered that I was Irish, and that I liked poetry, she insisted on buying me a double whiskey. Things were getting better by the hour. Sipping my whiskey with Miss Jamaica by my side, and a gloomy looking Chinese girl watching proceedings from across the bar, gave me an awesome sense of power.

Jez, I could have a harem by the time the class term finishes.

Now that would be something to boast about during a darts match in my local in Cork. When I hit the 'Mens' Room' I spent a considerable amount of time in front of the mirror trying to establish where all this sex appeal had suddenly come from – perhaps it was the birth of the baldy patch on my head that did the trick.

The more mature student…. The older the fiddle lark….

Sure enough, a lot had been written in the papers that the follicle-challenged, were in fact, the best lovers on this or any other planet. Whatever the reason I had it in spades anyway.

Miss Jamaica and me were laughing so much – the drink being responsible for most of it – we were almost chucked out of the watering hole. We were interfering with the more serious people who thought the café was just for eating and scowling. As she moved closer to me and placed her hand in mine I could smell her perfume, and feel the silkiness of her skin. My Chinese friend was not too pleased with this, and she upped sail and went her way, but not before inviting me to a party on the Saturday night. I told her I would consult my diary and be in touch with her. Inside every good man is a miserable bollocks and I was becoming that bollocks in record time. My popularity did not go astray on Miss Jamaica; she hastily booked me for drinks, and whatever else, for Friday night. Better get in early, I could be snapped up.   Just like when Ireland went through its golden age – The Land of Saints and Scholars – it seemed to me that I was approaching some magnificent period in my life. But my period in the stratosphere was short lived. When I encountered Miss Jamaica near the college the following night, she was hanging out of an Italian stud. Italy was the flavour for that day and poor Ireland was well down the list. In class she relocated herself, and this feline creature from Jamaica spread herself very thinly in a very short time. She did indeed have a flavour every day, and seeing her around the college with every Tom, Dick and Mario somehow lessened her attractiveness. But my efforts to emulate James Bond were short-lived, and I got a right kick in the balls when it was richly deserved. My friendship with the petite Chinese girl went on to flourish and we remained great friends for a period, but like a lot of things in life, our lives moved into different avenues and I never saw her again.

Through a contact at Alliance I got myself a beautiful apartment near Parc de Prince, right on the borders of the Bois de Boulogne. There is no nicer place to experience the beautiful spring and summer days in Paris than roaming through the Bois de Boulogne.

Bliss was it in that dawn to be alive

But to be young was very heaven.

I loved the early morning runs. On Saturdays, I would rise around seven and go out to the Bois and run and walk for up to two hours, and by the time I get back to my apartment, I would have the sweat of a racehorse on my back. A steaming hot shower, followed up with a cold shower, would set me up for the day. After these runs, I felt so good in myself, that I really felt that there was nothing in the entire world that I could not conquer, if I put my mind to it. I was intoxicated with fresh air and freedom and ready for more adventure and discovery. My drill was always the same on Saturday mornings. Take off in the metro and the suburban trains and explore Paris and its environs with no plan of action and without consulting any maps – everything on the hoof. On one such day I took off, and could never have imagined in a million years what the day held in store for me. Having attended a street market for an hour or two, I had a bite of lunch, explored a few parks and then headed off to some other part of the city in the metro. Never quite knowing where I was in the city, kept my anticipation and adrenalin pumping.

Those were the days of our lives!

At some remote station I alighted from the metro, ambled up a few streets, hit a café and tried to establish my bearings. As it was pushing on in the evening, I decided that I might as well head back to my apartment, but first of all I had to figure out where the hell I was in Paris. I turned down a few streets only to notice that the landscape was getting grottier by the minute, and low and behold when I looked behind me, the path was filling up with undesirables who all seemed to be on my trail. When I looked to my front once more, my path there seemed to be blocked off as well. These guys were slowly approaching me and hemming me into a circle in a very menacing way. I had no option but to slip into a grotty café to avoid the trouble. From the frying pan into the fire – if the inhabitants of the road looked menacing the clientele of this place were absolutely terrifying. The men were scattered around on battered old seating, all swarthy and dangerous; the young women all brown-skinned and scantily dressed. I knew instantly I had strayed into a knocking shop and that my kind was not welcomed here. I was certain my life was in danger as I stood at the counter almost shitting myself on the spot from the sheer terror of it all. One or two of the bunch were edging towards me; quickly I called for a ricard for myself and for the guy next to me at the counter. The barman shook his head.

"No English serve here."

Glad of the opportunity I jumped in straight away.

"I'm Irish. Irelande … Dublin … Belfast … Bang, bang, bang!"

He moved slowly towards the end of the bar, his head bent forward as if he was assessing the situation. Finally a nod from one of the guys at the end of the bar gave him the go-ahead to serve me.

"OK, just … one," he went for the ricard bottle and measure.

I knew from the conversation he was having with the others that he was not happy with me, but he poured the one drink and instantly put his hand out for the money. This was very unusual, but I knew there was no welcome for me in this North African café.

I had a dilemma.

Would I finish my drink and head out to the danger lurking outside, or would I risk delaying on here, and maybe build some kind of rapport with the people in the café. Either way I was in grave danger.

The words of my father were spinning round in my head.

"Always keep a cool head, and always be full of surprises – it knocks everyone off kilter."

If ever I needed to heed those words it was now.

I could feel the eyes on the back of my head as I stood by the counter; I was half-afraid to lift the glass to my mouth for fear they would see my hand shaking.

So for me it was grab your courage, down the drink in one go and launch the surprise. Instantly I called on the barman to fill the same again for me and give a drink to all at the counter, and before he could say another word I burst into song:

"O Danny Boy, the pipes, the pipes are calling."

They were flummoxed!

I continued right down to the last verse of the song, blasting away like a demented lunatic; and just as I was about to finish

"And I shall live in peace until you come ... to ... me ..."

I turned to the gang behind me, spread my arms, and bowed.

The cheer went up.

A nutcase is accepted in every culture.

Music, like love, had conquered all.

I started a fire. The sombre mood lifted. The Big Chief at the end of the counter was more amused than most and burst open a few bottles of decent rouge. The ladies came alive at the sight of the free booze and jazzed up as if their batteries had been recharged. For the first time in my life, I had witnessed a real substantial metamorphosis. It took a mad Irishman who was frightened out of his skin to light the fuse under these particular patrons, and as it turned out it sparked a great night. Plates of couscous were placed before me, I was plied with wine and calvados and beer and the devil knows what, until it was time to shut up shop for the night. It was three o'clock in the morning before I left the premises. One of the gang rang his brother-in-law, who was a taxi driver, to bring me home; and I travelled the ten mile journey, happy as a pig in shit after a most extraordinary day.

And to crown it all, the driver refused to take the fare.

One up for our North Africans brothers.

This was my great piece of luck: that I escaped that night with my life. And another bit of good luck, though trivial by comparison, was the fact that I had a pad on the edge of the Bois de Boulogne. The Bois is a wonderful park located along the western edge of the 16th arrondissement of Paris; and covers more than two thousand acres; and is two and half times bigger than Central Park in New York; and three times larger than Hyde Park in London. And as the spring turned into summer, I spent more and more time in that magnificent setting. There was always more to explore. From all the training and activity I was getting very fit, so-much-so, that I decided to run to work in the mornings through the bois, a journey of about six miles. When I would hit my place of work, about eight in the morning, the sweat would pour out of me like a bad Kerry shower – avoirdupois was not a word in my lexicon then. A hot shower followed by a cold one and this old bucko was set up for the day. And every day brought me to a new location in the city and with a different bunch of workmates; this day we happen to be working in the Colombes district of Paris when I encountered the complete mutton head of the lowest life in France. On my crew was a thick skulled man who seemed to spend half his life flexing his muscles. He was one of those people who was nasty to everyone, from getting up in the morning to him going to bed at night. And so he was with me all the morning on the job. We were doing a tough shift, lugging heavy machinery about. By lunchtime, every muscle in my body was aching, and I relished the chance to sit down in the café and have lunch. The crew had the customary bottle of vin rouge and all was well with the world. As I was paying my bill I got into conversation with the owner of the café – a fleshy woman with blue hair and a broad smile. When she discovered that I was Irish we got into a long discussion about her travels in Ireland, and she knew Ireland pretty well having visited the country on many occasions. She spoke about the Gap of Dunloe, the dangers of kissing the Blarney Stone – especially for a woman of her proportions – and how she loved the craic in the pubs in the west of Ireland. She was having a right old chin wag, her cheeks dancing in her face as she relived her visits to Ireland. Before I was ready to go, she threw a calvados in front of me – a treat from the café. By now, the crew all fortified with the rouge, were ready for another afternoon of lifting. We each paid our bills and I left a tip on the little plate – my tip was a little over the odds for a lunch but what the hell. Muscle man had his eye on the plate and picked up half the money I had left and refused point blank to return it to the plate.

"It's too much."

"Listen," I said in my best French, "I'll decide that," my anger growing.

He put the money in his pocket, to the amusement of the other workmates. My shackles were now rising in earnest, as I ordered him to put the money back. At this stage he knew how angry I was, but he still persisted to hold on to the money. I knew the bastard wanted the money for himself and that he had already calculated that he was dealing with an old mug that would give up easily.

"For the final time, put the money back on the plate."

By now I was shouting and the clients of the café were all tuned in; the owner had by this stage moved just in front of us. The muscle man had nowhere to hide and he did not want to lose face with the gang. He put his hand in his pocket, took out the money and dropped in into my coffee. That did it. I picked up the scalding hot black coffee and let him have it straight in the face.

"That will wipe the fucking smile off your face," now I was shouting in English.

The owner's eyes lit up and doubled in size, and her face reddened to boiling point. Muscle man was screaming but made no attempt at retaliating. When I had gathered myself and got some bit of control back in my head, I apologised to the lady for upsetting her and the customers. The muscle man turned out not to be too badly burned, but one thing for sure, he never crossed my path again, and he dampened down any ambitions that others in the crew might have had in that direction. I suppose the other workmates realised that I was a loyal friend but a deadly enemy; either way it was totally out of character for me to behave like that.

Sometimes we are as different from ourselves as we are from other people!

But those nasty incidents were forgotten about and very shortly I was considered one of the crew – I had earned my stirrups. And the management gave me recognition as well – a hefty pay rise and an invitation to dinner in The Big Chief's house. This was a rare occurrence in Paris, for a foreigner to be invited to the home of the Managing Director. So on the Saturday night, I decked myself out in my Joseph coat, my new black trousers, and my high rise shoes that raised me about six inches off the ground – I could have been a member of New York Globetrotters.

The Citroen pulled up and my host taxied me away to the suburbs. He was a man who smiled a lot for a Parisian, and had the wet look ever before it became poplar. Arriving at his apartment, his wife greeted me with a firm handshake and the immortal lines,

"We have a special meal for you tonight … l'escargots."

In any language, that sounded a disaster to me – how the fuck was I going to eat snails. The first part of my plan was to get as much alcohol into my system, as quickly as possible; and to have an aperitif because I was in France; followed by a stiff whiskey because I was Irish; and plenty of the vin rouge because I was about to eat snails. The pair looked at me agog! Of course everyone in Ireland drinks at that pace – I'm only doing what comes naturally to us Celts. Eventually the offending objects were put in front of me on the table and through a haze I gazed at the little fuckers – curried if you don't mind.

"More wine?" called out the hostess now speaking in English.

I topped up again and gave one almighty gulp just before I did the deed. By this stage the master of the house was waxing lyrical about the lads on the plate, and I was trying to remember what continent I was on. Before I hit the salad, never mind the fromage I was fast asleep on the chair with the escargots well and truly secured in the belly. When I woke and realised the horrible situation I had put myself into, and realised what a bollocks I made of myself, and how I had disgraced my country: there was nothing for it but to come clean and verbalise my absolute fear about the little lads on the plate and how it had drove me to drink at such an alarming rate. My host and hostess said they were very glad that I did not drink like that on a daily basis, and that I was very brave soul to confess my fears – they thought I was a true champion. I had climbed many notches in their estimation of me and they promised me that they would have Irish strew on the menu the next time I would darken their door. But I never did again, for soon afterwards I quit the job and became a full time student (dosser) at Alliance Francaise. From now on I would be spending more time in the beautiful Luxembourg Gardens – Le Jardin du Luxembourg – surrounded by the most beautiful girls in all of Paris.

'Ill - weaved ambition, how much are thou shrunk'

The plan was terrific. Take myself to the college in the morning after my early gallop, have a leisurely lunch with the other students, and take myself off to the Luxembourg gardens to laze away the afternoons. It was a consoling and refreshing thought that the French Government were helping to pay for my Bohemian existence by subsidising my lunch – for this I would pledge my everlasting love for all things French into the future. On a beautiful sunny day, there is nowhere else on earth that I would rather be than hanging around those magnificent gardens. They had a unique atmosphere created by the beautiful lakes, the wonderful statues, the funny capped bowl players and those lush greens, the beautiful array of multi-coloured flowers and the many buskers and madcap bands that were scattered throughout the gardens. On the park benches, we talked about who was around and in control of the outfit before God appeared, and whether Communism had ever a realistic chance to prosper, and if Einstein could change a flat tyre on a car – as you can see, all practical questions. But the more important questions, like who had the best pair of legs or the best tits at Alliance were more hotly debated. We did not like the females to be in on the discussions, for they were far too practical for us males. But there was one female, who was almost always in on the discussions, and she hailed from Sweden. Now ninety–nine times out of a hundred you would be correct to imagine a blonde bombshell, but alas, in this case it was not so – a pity for it was my good self that was the object of her affections.

And she wasted no time in letting me know. No beating about the bush with Inger.

She wanted an Irishman and as I was the only one there in the flesh, she attached her emotions to me. She was a large woman for a twenty-year-old: she had the Swedish blonde hair that was always bobbed to same level with her ears; she had two cheeks on her face as large as those on her arse; and she wore a pair of spectacles with lenses as wide and as thick as a garden glasshouse. She spoke about a hundred and four languages, her IQ was said to be the highest ever recorded in Sweden – and she was madly in love with me.

What did I ever do to deserve this?

One day when my money had run out, and when I was starved to the point where the crows in the Luxembourg Gardens were eyeing me up, I accepted an invitation to go to lunch with her. She was generous, and indeed charming, far beyond the call of duty. We had the full shebang lunch in a beautiful restaurant off the Boulevard St. Michel – aperitifs, the best Bordeaux in the house, starters, main course, desert, and chasers of all descriptions – I did not intend getting hungry for at least another week. She invited me back to her apartment in Montparnasse, but I declined saying that I was knackered and that I had a major exam the next day. So I jumped on the metro, and headed home to devour the last of the few bottles of beer I had in the fridge, before hitting the sack early. I had more luck than an honest man, for when I rose in the morning there was the envelope with the big cheque inside – my bloody tax rebate from Ireland. I said the first prayer in the history of the world for the revenue people as I hotfooted down to the bank to cash the cheque.

Is there a God there or what?

Soon I was back on the bench with the gang and spondulux in my phoca – the best feeling in the world.   I pretended to Inger that the exam had been postponed, and that I had picked up a few bob on loan from one of the mates at the complex. I had no intention of letting her know that I was flush with cash in fear she might be demanding a rebate for the millions she had spent the evening before – but she was not a vindictive person, and after all, her old man was a multi-millionaire – she also told me that the day before. But hanging around the college and gardens every day got a bit boring and I needed to work because the pile was diminishing at an alarming rate. Unfortunately, the only job I could pick up demanded that I work a full day, so I had to resign from my studies for a period while I was replenishing the francs.   I got a crappy and boring job in a factory not far from the Arc, parcelling up orders to be sent to the four corners of the country. There was an old guy working with me, who had been doing that same job well before the invasion of Paris by the Nazis. He showed me the exact spot he stood on, all those years previously, when he watched the troops come into the city. Though I was bowled over by that fact, I was more bowled over when he told me that it took him two and a half hours to come to work each day by train and the same to return home. I spent about two months or so in that job, which I found utterly boring, but one funny incident happened to me when returning home to my apartment one evening. I was passing Parc de Prance on the day that the French Cup final was taking place. Obviously I had no tickets for the match, when suddenly this big black car pulled up beside me – I was quickly surrounded by a large bunch of police who seemed to drop out of the air. I was held within the cordon, as the door of the black car was flung open, and out steps Giscard D'Eisteng – The President of France. The gate into the stadium opened as if by magic and we were on our way to the match – the President and myself. It appeared to me that the police thought that I was one of the special branch protecting the president by the respect they seemed to be showing to me. We were ushered into our prime seats and I sat behind ~~the~~ Le President for the entire game even though I was terrified to open my mouth least they find out that I was an impostor – and I could end up in a strange place with a knee on my chest. Before the match was over, I skedaddled during the excitement to another area of the stand, and made my exit in my own time. When I returned home I was reflecting on the farcical security situation with the President when I heard a strange voice on the intercom.

Jez, it was Inger – how the hell did she find out where I lived?

I opened the door for her and she was about to recite her undying love for me when I put my hand in the air and I began to speak.

"It's like this Inger, I have a wife and triplets at home in Ireland and it would not be a clever idea to start a relationship."

I came over to France to learn French rapidly as my wife and myself were about to open a pub in West Cork and the majority of the patrons would be French.

It worked.

We agreed to stay friends and I promised to look her up when I returned to the college in the coming weeks. We had a drink or two and I heard her mumbling to herself as she descended the stairs.

"Triplets, imagine that!"

When I encountered Inger again in the Luxembourg Gardens she was hooked up with a French teacher from Cavan; who was over at Alliance Francaise to brush up on his French. She was full of the joys of spring and never even asked me how the triplets were getting on – she had moved to new pastures and it was now The

Cavan Man who was representing the manhood of Ireland. But as I concentrated more on my studies, I lost contact with the happy couple, and some time later I heard that they announced their engagement – I knew then for sure that the Cavan Man got wind of the vast fortune behind Inger.

My exams complete, and with my lease on the apartment running out, it was time to turn my head once more towards the Emerald shore – But God nor man could not have foretold what was in store for me when I returned home.

CHAPTER FOUR

I was in my twenties when I first got a taste of real disappointment, and it happened in the most bizarre fashion imaginable. I had just returned from Paris having spent a year in that fantastic city studying French at the Alliance Francaise. When I hit Cork after my sojourn abroad, I was in the best shape of my life having trained for most days in the Bois de Boulogne. I was looking forward to returning to Paris to complete my French exams, while also hoping to compete in some athletic meetings in that wonderful city. But life intervenes when we are planning something else. I was involved in a weird accident, and I would surmise, that one would have a better chance of winning the Lotto two weeks in a row than having this accident. I was sauntering through Daunts Square when this fellow took a tumble on the footpath. I reached out to catch him but he slipped down under my grip and his full weight came crashing down on my ankle. The crack from my leg could be heard a hundred yards away. Soon I was speeding in an ambulance towards the North Infirmary feeling every bump that the Cork streets threw up. The next time I encountered this world again was when I woke up in intensive care. The surgeon's voice was sombre, as was the news. Four breaks in my ankle with the same number of bones displaced.

And the excruciating pain confirmed that fact.

Though I was heavily sedated the slightest movement sent hot needles of pain shooting through my body. Eventually I gave up the ghost and mercifully slid into some drug-induced sleep.

After a few days ranging from half awareness to complete oblivion, I was transferred to the Male Surgical Ward. The haze was lifting but the pain was just as intense. The nurses would hold back on issuing the strong painkillers, and would only allow me one in extreme circumstances. This was the practice at the time – the fear being that one might get immune to the tablets, and if that should happen there was nothing left in the armoury to curtail the outrageous pain. At the time I would have taken my chances – in fact I would do almost anything to escape from the excruciating pain. My new ward with its smoky-yellow walls and high ornate ceiling would be my hellhole for the foreseeable future. As I lay in my hospital bed I pondered on the freakishness of the accident and how shaggin' unlucky I was to be in that spot at that time – I must have run the picture sequence a thousand times in my head. Each time I could hear again the almighty crack as his entire weight landed on my ankle, and the same dead feeling, as if the bottom half of my leg had been severed. And that pain; surging through my body like a fire out of control. And I remembered something else – the guy that fell on me had no hands. Christ that's how I was unable to get a grip on him and bit-by-bit the picture was coming together in my head. I was unable to get a grip on him so he slipped through my hands: my foot slid onto the roadway just off the path and the crushing weight of his body trapped my ankle between the road and the path. Is it any wonder we were talking major damage. He scampered off leaving me writhing in pain.

Such is the reward for the good deed!

Welcome to the Black Hole of Calcutta – or The North Infirmary.

I was in my mid-twenties with no job, no money, no chance of finishing my studies in Paris, and with very little prospects of walking in the foreseeable future if ever again – and yes my athletic career was ended.

And always that pain – morning, noon and night – there was no escape.

It was family and friends that egged me on each day to keep some kind of a spirit going. They were awful days and awful nights and times when I could have lifted off the glass dome ceiling of the ward if I could verbalise my pain and my hurt.

After my second operation, and with a cast in place on my leg the savage pain began to recede somewhat and I could now shuffle round the bed a little bit better. This improvement continued and I knew I was returning to the real world when I began to notice the nurses, or should I say notice their legs. The nurses wore white uniforms and many wore the shortest of skirts, which did more to aid recuperation than a bucket of medicine. It was just as well we had such pleasant companionship in the ward, for I was booked in for a long stay. The other inmates of the ward were making themselves known in various ways and – it seemed to me – were intent on squeezing some fun from their unfortunate plight. Chief among those was a tearaway nicknamed Compensation and he got this name for obvious reasons.

I first encountered Compensation's voice even before I had a glimpse of his bald white skull and plump red face. Although still in his early thirties, he was aging badly and at a rapid rate to boot. Around this period Abba had a huge hit with 'Money, Money, Money' and this anthem was adopted by Compensation as his theme song for the duration of his stay. He continued to subject the patients in the ward to his dreadful rendition every night of the week. Everyone in the ward knew the story how a bus rolled over his leg, and for Compensation this was the best piece of luck he had since he was born.

"Get the fucking money ready."

He would shout out whenever the sister left the room. The sister was christened Hitler, not only because she possessed the same tyrannical approach as her namesake, but also as she had more than a hint of a black moustache. Compensation was crafty enough not to cross her, for he could find himself out on his arse if she ever heard him use that kind of bad language in the ward. When Hitler would recite the rosary in the evening to the captured audience, the one voice that could be heard towering above the rest was the lilting voice of Compensation. This guy brought hypocrisy to another level. When the consultant, with his medical students in tow, would visit Compensation on his daily walk-round, Compensation would lay in the bed like a frightened mouse pretending to be all coy and shy. But as soon as the Hippocratic God would disappear out the door of the ward the war cry would rise up

"Get the fucking money ye bollocks."

The other inmates – short on excitement – would rattle the metal frames of the beds, until a cacophony of sound would envelop the entire ward. One would never guess that each and every bed was holding a sick person. San Quentin had nothing on this place. During my early weeks in The Male Surgical it was Compensation who hugged the limelight, due to the fact that he shouted the loudest. When the doctor told him that his leg would not be amputated, he was the most disappointed man in the County of Cork.

"Jesus Christ, a man has no luck when he has an open and closed case."

But The Echo Boy – another inmate of the famous ward – had no such luck. Even though he was known as 'The Echo Boy' he was in fact a man in his seventies. The Echo Boy had his leg removed, and having spent a week or so in the intensive care he was returned to his cronies in the ward. His pain was so severe that his voice would fill the entire ward with his screaming and even the strongest medication did little to ease the awful pain. It was the kind of screaming that would wake the dead. On one occasion Hitler told him there was a bed in Heaven for him, before tucking her veil to one side and speeding away.

Fucking sure there is, I thought to myself.

I had a visit from a friend who thought it a nice gesture to bring me a dozen pint bottles of Guinness – though my leg was damaged my mouth was still intact. Not familiar with the routine of the hospital my friend placed the bottles under the bed.

Mistake!

The next morning was clean-up day. Everything in sight was washed, cleaned or dusted under the watchful eye of Hitler herself. When my bed was wheeled out of position all hell broke loose. Tall and proud stood the dozen stout bottles; naked for all to see. The nurses tried to hide them but Hitler had an eye like a hawk. She came at me in the bed, her large frame shaking with rage and a face that would have sent Sonny Liston scurrying for cover.

"How did these bottles get under your bed?"

I had nowhere to hide –

"Someone must have put them under my bed when I was asleep."

Her face got even redder.

"Nurse, get those bottles out of here immediately."

With one final scowl in my direction, she scurried off leaving the frantic cleaning to the nurses. That evening when the coast was clear, and the good nun was tucked warmly up in her bed, a pair of nurses returned the stout bottles, and I had my first creamy pint in hospital. I passed around the bottles to the thirsty mouths and we finished the full complement that evening.

When the Guinness hit the medication we were spifo in our beds, and before the clock struck midnight we were in full chorus, and the sounds drifted out the windows of the Male Surgical down passed the ears of the passers-by on Infirmary Road, and they must have wondered on that night that we were the happiest patients in all the world. As Johnny Smiley was the only one in the ward able to get about, he was detailed to collect the evidence and dispose of the empty bottles before any danger appeared.

There was a young guy next to me in the ward who had broken his leg playing football and each evening his sister came to visit him. She was a nun and always wore her habit. Before departing each evening she would say a prayer with him, and as soon as the nun departed the scene, this nurse would appear from out of thin air, pull the blinds round his bed and take herself in beside our young stag. Despite the cast on his leg there would be more huffing and puffing emanating from behind those blinds than you would ever hear in the Moulin Rouge. When the business of the evening was completed the nurse would pull the blinds, the young stag would wink in my direction, and the nurse would go about her business in a nonchalant manner. The bloody thing was contagious, for two weeks later his sister – the praying nun – shagged off with the parish priest who was another frequent visitor to the young stag. The two were never heard of again.

When I related the story to Old Jack in the ward, he just shrugged his shoulders and uttered in his inimitable way:

"Sure, isn't there plenty of it there" It took me a while to figure that one out.

Those were the good old days when smoking was allowed in hospitals, and each evening when all the Hippocratic Knobs had deserted the hospital I lit up my pipe. When the lights would be dropped for the night I would often light up, lay back on the pillow and wonder how the fuck did I manage to get myself in here.

Inside our little world in the Male Surgical, as the days tumbled into weeks, we got to know each other pretty well. Compensation had his third operation and difficulties set in, and he was the happiest man in the world.

The Mummy arrived in the middle of the night bandaged from head to foot. The nurses said he had fallen from a roof onto a pile of concrete bricks; from his outside packaging it looked as if every bone in his body was broken. He had more hoses and equipment attached to him than a Ferrari Racing Car. Compensation looked at him with an envious eye.

"There's easily a million in that for him if he survives" he explained to the ward.

The Mummy didn't open an eye for five days and five nights. The priest was called on two occasions and the prayers for the dead were said but he still battled on.

The first visible signs that the Mummy was going to stay on this side of the grave came one afternoon when he raised a hand.

I stumbled to his side.

His voice was barely audible, but I recognised the word 'smoke'.

"Jesus, he wants a smoke."

I cried out to the assembled multitude.

"That will really kill the fucker"shouted Compensation.

Here give the poor bastard a fag," came a voice from the other side. A box of Sweet Afton was thrown in my direction. I took a fag and placed it where I suspected his mouth might be – I lit the fag and soon there was smoke bellowing in and out of the slit. He almost suffocated with the first few puffs, but I held the fag steady between my fingers and the Mummy got his rhythm going and floated into another heaven.

I had a new job.

Though the Mummy was a great surprise and source of entertainment for the inmates, our next patient could have come straight from the forests of Borneo. A team of nurses and junior doctors delivered him into the ward. All we could see was a crop of thick matted dirty black hair on top, and below a pair of well-worn waders – a strange sight to behold anywhere but especially in a hospital setting. When the accompanying medical team tried to hoist him on to the bed he let out a screech louder and more frightening than any Kerry banshee. Nurse Malone, who was as strong as an ox caught him under the arse, and with her other hand lifted him on to the bed. But this bucko continued to roar that there was nothing wrong with him. The doctor tried to pacify him, but it was the nurses who soon took command of the situation. Nurse Malone turned to me and murmured that she would soon put an end to his antics with a good needle in the arse – that would put the quieteners on him.

And it did.

"Get the bastard to the bath and scrub the bollocks off him now," is how Nurse Malone put it. He was returned to the ward some hours later, spanking clean from his trip to the bath, but the hairy bastard was still protesting. But another jab near the Magillacuddy Reeks and he soon fell deep into the arms of Morpheus, or so we thought. During the night I heard a strange noise coming from Banshee's bed, which was right next to my own.

"Lishen boyeen, he whispered in my direction, would you ever keep an eye on my boots (the waders) if I fall asleep ... all my life savings are in there."

It transpired that he had a thousand pounds stuffed into the waders, but there was no need for me to keep an eye on them, for he did not close an eye for the entire night and he held a fixed gaze on the waders all night. When I related the story to Compensation about the money in the waders he swore he would seriously harm himself for passing up such an opportunity. But the wild Banshee was not destined to be long with us – no, he did not shuffle off the mortal coil – he was discharged, waders and all the following morning. All hell broke loose in the hospital when it was learned that the wrong man had been admitted. A phone call to the hospital revealed that the Banshee's brother was the one that should have been admitted – both men lived in the same house and the ambulance men picked up the wrong man. Nurse Malone said that it appeared that the brother was higher up the madness chain than the Banshee and that they both should be brought to a more secure location – like the lunatic asylum.

Despite the frequent laughs and crazy situations, The Male Surgical changed me forever. A couple of months on the flat of your back is a harrowing experience to cope with for a start. The very best prognosis for me was that I would walk in twelve months with a limp – that was with luck, and provided that I had all the necessary physiotherapy. Long term I may lose the limp in another twelve months or so. My athletic career was over, and the chance of me returning to Paris and completing my studies was unlikely. My ambition to go to the Sorbonne was truly dead. I was in my mid-twenties, crocked and flat broke. When the intense pain died away, it was then that the real anger set in. I cursed the living daylights out of the guy I saved on that footpath in Daunts Square; though my anger died away somewhat when I learned later that he had his own problems to deal with; he was born without any hands. Over the months in the Male Surgical, I had witnessed some dreadful scenes and something fundamental was taking place deep down in my being. Seeing the courage of others, and seeing the dignity and patience they showed through the most harrowing experiences made me a mellower person; and much more willing to forgive and to forget.

And during the process, I had learned a little word called empathy.

Someday I would have to brush myself down, try and pick up the pieces and move forward with a brand new set of dreams.

But, be I happy or sad, life went on apace in the hospital.

Practically the same crew were still on board. Compensation was holding meetings on a regular basis with his legal team behind closed blinds, and I was holding the fag steady for the Mummy who was now up to ten-a-day and rising.

Hitler went away to some convent for a vacation, to recharge her turbo, and the smiles came back on the faces of the nurses. Sometime later, a rumour was circulating that Hitler had run away with another woman – we all thought that this woman had to be the bravest woman in the entire world. But they must have been some credence in the gossip for the plump face of the holy sister never darkened the walls of the Male Surgical again. The most beautiful nun one would ever lay eyes on replaced her, and she had the personality to go with it. The crocks in the ward fell instantly in love with her – we became the new apostles of voyeurism – and we had the time on our hands to perfect that art. Her smile and sheer style lit up the ward and dispersed any of the lingering gloom left over since Hitler's departure.

We were happy campers for the most part and I was improving having had two further operations. Being able to leave my bed and go by myself to the toilet was better than winning the Nobel Prize … things were looking up.

I started writing humorous poems incorporating all the idiosyncratic behaviour I saw around me; and every Friday night I would recite my poems for the motley collection. It was great fun and everyone looked forward to our little diversion from the tedium of hospital life. Even when I included very intimate private details about the crew it never met with any disapproval. My fame as Ireland's greatest living poet was spreading throughout the hospital to such an extent, that they began to call me 'The Mad Poet of the Male Surgical'.

But poets have their bad days too – probably more than most. A wet November day comes to mind, with the rain beating an everlasting tattoo on the large windowpanes. Not alone was the Black Dog on my back, but all his family. It was typical of hospital life – all would appear to be going well, when suddenly out of the blue, this mist would descend. This particular day was an in-between day. I was unhappy in bed but did not want to be up and about; I wanted to read but did not have the concentration; I was half alive but I wouldn't have minded being dead. It was a day when time is visible in the quarter-second.

Thankfully that evening my mind was switched to a new patient who was placed next to my own bed. From his accompanying entourage it was obvious that he was a rural man; for his family spoke with country accents. As the evening was drawing in, I could see the silhouettes of the medical staff dancing on the screens as they worked to make the patient as comfortable as possible – his family had temporarily left, only to return when the screens were opened up again.

When tea was being served all visitors had to leave the hospital; the rain stopped and calmness descended. Eight o'clock again would see an invasion by the outside world – the last event for the day. I was glad to see the back of the visitors for I could now settle down with my pipe to some serious smoking without a murmur of protest. Following the usual ritual of cutting the tobacco from the plug, rolling it in my palms to achieve the right consistency, filling the pipe with the exact pressure, the crack of the match and the first long pull on the pipe signalled that all was right with the world again. Settled back on the pillow and sending white smoke upwards to the high ceiling. I could have been back in my grandfather's house once more, finding and naming the animals in the smoke.

The eyes of my new neighbour were firmly fixed on me, his head resting to the side and his white hair spilling over the pillow. Not a word spoken. The night drew on and the lights of the ward were dropped further for the night. The steely eyes were still firmly fixed on me. I hadn't the slightest touch of sleep about me so I lit up once more. The first puff drew a response; he raised a hand and in the faintest whisper uttered something in my direction. I left my bed and went to his side.

"Would you ever be so kind and loan me a fill of tobacco, forgot to bring my own with me."

"Get your pipe out there and we'll have you steaming in no time," I uttered.

He puffed to his heart's content, and his expression assumed an air of calmness, until finally, he raised his hand once more letting me know that he wished to put his pipe away.

He turned on his side, and calmly left this world behind.

He died before my eyes.

The feelings and the images of that night burned deep into my consciousness, and those images were still so vivid many years later, that I wrote a little poem to keep the moment alive forever.

NORTH INFIRMARY 1974

Old man,
I never knew your name
Yet, I sent you to your Maker
With the smell of my tobacco
On your breath.
You must have loved that pipe
For at dead of night
In our shadowy hospital ward
You summoned up the courage
To ask me for a fill,
I packed your pipe
Full of the warmest Erinmore.
You thanked me with your hand

And slowly, you lit up a little piece of heaven
For yourself
As you drew in that first long smoke.
At four you signaled me
To put your pipe away
And when you held my hand
I knew your strength had gone.
Before first milking you departed
..........Leaving behind a young man
Warm, that in lonely hours
Lit a tiny halo on an old man's pipe.

CHAPTER FIVE

We had the biggest lunatic asylum in the world in Cork in the 'sixties. The official asylum ran parallel to the river Lee – a magnificent stone edifice that seemed to run on for miles and dominate the skyline over the river. It had bars on all the windows. The unofficial madhouse was situated in the Marina and had no bars on the windows, but it had a name over the door 'Henry Ford and Son Ltd'.

I had returned from London in late 'sixty-six with the objective of going to UCC, but a neighbour who called a lot of the shots at the afore mentioned company, suggested I go for an interview for a 'great job' in Industrial Relations.

Surprise, surprise, the job was offered to me a week later, and I almost pissed in my pants when I saw the starting salary – it was huge – so I said yes.

Prior to starting in the job, I played a football game in the county championship on the Sunday and broke my two fingers during the game, so I started the job with a lump of plaster all the way up to my elbow. No-one seemed to give a hoot that it was also my writing hand – I was plunked behind a desk and told to "get on and learn the fucking job". They were the precise words.

And I did.

At that time, there were fifteen hundred employees – as distinct from workers – within the boundary walls of the motor company. Whether it was the repetitive nature of assembly work, or whether Fords drew lunatics and general freaks as a matter of course, was never established, but these oddballs were scattered throughout the workforce in generous numbers. And Prince among them, was known to all and sundry, as 'The Cock', for obvious reasons. 'The Cock', in his working clothes, was a tall angular man with a long aquiline nose and tossed long hair – he would not look out of place stuck in some orchestral pit – but in Fords he operated from the trimline and made music of a different kind – birdlike.

Many a dull Monday morning would come to life when 'The Cock', would give it full throttle – from the shell of a cortina or an escort would come the most perfect "cock-a-doodle-doo" that would reverberate right throughout the factory floor.

The response from the other workers would be spontaneous and noisy. A cacophony of sound emanating from metal on metal would saturate the entire factory, and the sound would only encourage 'The Cock' to even louder bellows. The Production Manager listening in his office knew that all production had now ceased, and that all hell was breaking out on the factory floor, would head for the trim line promising to choke the fucking cock as soon as he laid eyes on him. But the bush telegraph would issue the warning along the line and 'The Cock' would be beavering like fuck at his job as soon as Mr Big appeared. Some time and motion people in Ford would agree, that in fact 'The Cock' was good for production, as he raised the spirits of the workers in boring monotonous jobs; but Mr Big promised that if he ever caught him 'cock-a-doodling', he would personally choke him with his bare hands on the spot. Outside of the factory floor in Fords, 'The Cock' was destined for greater things. Some of his workmates got wind of a talent contest in Carrigaline, where the winner was decided by the applause generated for the individuals in the hall. The 'Cock' went into special practise for the event. By this stage 'The Cock' had gone completely lampy – he insisted that he 'cock-a doodled' better that any real cock in Ireland – it was white coat time. On the night of the contest he was led into the hall by a lone piper with a couple of hundred of his fellow workers in train. After his performance of 'The Cock-A-Doodle-Doo', the applause that followed could have won him an Olympic medal, never mind a talent contest, and he duly collected first prize.

His performances at work grew louder and more frequent after his victory, and it took a stiff letter from the company warning him that he would soon find himself 'cock-a-doodling' at the Labour Exchange if he continued to disrupt the entire production at the factory. That brought some semblance of order to the whole affair.

The 'Cock' had a companion in the trim line who was another source of worry for the Production Management Team – a wizen-faced little devil that needed constant attention. Fords, like all big companies at the time had their own surgery, staffed by a doctor and nurse. The doctor would visit the sick employees most days of the week which left the surgery in the care of the male nurse. 'Wizen-Face', had the eye of a hawk; for as soon as the surgery was empty he would strike and head straight for the mentholated spirits. He would put the bottle to his head and hey presto the white poison would disappear down the hatch. From eight o'clock on Monday morning, to closing time on Friday, 'Wizen-Face' lived for that fix, watching for his opportunity to pounce. He had being doing it for years, and despite several warnings and suspensions; the company had never acted to toft him out.

Oh the mystery that is management.

And one day they got the opportunity to improve the management – it came in the person of one tall, lean and continuously smiling black man. He arrived at the Labour Relations Office following a phone call from the security at the front gate that Martin Luther King was on his way up to see us. I was the first to greet him.

He had worked as a senior manager in finance for the Ford organisation in America and Australia and was now looking for a foothold in Europe, and he liked the idea of working in Ireland. He had a briefcase full of testimonials and references from diverse quarters. I had a quick glance at the accompanying papers and even from a cursory look it was evident that this man could put a person on the moon.

But I was unable to get anyone to talk to him – the finance people thought the Personnel Manager should interview him but he was always busy with the union people, and he did not want to know. After two coffees and a half a packet of biscuits later, I got an older member of the Industrial Relations Staff to have a word with him – and we were listening in the adjoining room. After preliminaries, our man asked Luther if he had any relatives in Ireland. Now we are talking about a period in the sixties where the sight of a black man walking up Western Road to attend UCC caused the youngsters to follow him – this is how rare the sight of any black man was in Cork at the time. Luther laughingly dismissed the question by simply saying he was still looking in the Kerry area. But the comedy was to continue. Luther, not missing the opportunity to reel off his achievements, listed the universities he attended in America and continued to produce the necessary documentation to prove it – he was a great man for the paper. Our man was stumped in the presence of greatness and had nothing to say to Luther and in a mad moment went on to tell him that if he joined the company in Cork, he would have to join the Conquer Cancer Campaign, and that three pence a week would be stopped from his pay. That did it for us as we fell about the place in laughter.

"Would someone go in and rescue that man for Christ sake before any more damage is done," said the office cleaner. But as none of us was in a fit state to look Luther in the eye without cracking up,

I'm afraid he had to endure the awful interview for another few minutes. Eventually he emerged from the room, the smile now dead on his face, and replaced with a quizzical look as if he had totally lost his bearings. My manager instructed me to take him across to the finance people and see what they could make of him.

"For Christ sake, take him somewhere, but get him out of here."

I duly obeyed orders and headed with Luther for the finance building, to be interviewed now by Bill, the Accounts Manager. I duly dispatched him and waited in the very large open-plan office outside. Now this office contained the hard men of the Ford organisation – and the very nature of their work meant that any little deviation from figures was greatly welcomed. All eyes were on Luther and Bill.

Now Bill processed a very nervous disposition, and having risen through the ranks from general worker to Accounts Manager, had trained himself to be cautious – and he constantly looked over his shoulder to see who was coming up behind: in the jungle one had to be careful. It was only in times like these, that we appreciated the glass panelling for we could see every move, every glance and gesture. Bill's jaw was dropping as each minute passed; Luther, who at last had a willing listener, gave it the full welley; he was pulling papers from his briefcase quicker than any magician.

A half an hour later Bill stumbled to his feet, and muttered something, which brought a flashing smile to Luther's face. He gathered his testimonials, hurried right past me and straight out of the office.

One of the hardshaws shouted at Bill as soon as Luther disappeared out the door:

"Are you giving him a job Bill?"

"I am in my bollucks, he'd be setting in my chair next week."

I don't think we were quite ready to embrace the world. A company as big as Fords, which had been operating before the state was established, tends to develop a culture of its own. Good and bad practises grew up over the years, and one such practice was the passing on from worker-to-worker of soft pornography magazines that came into Fords from the big bad continent of Europe. The ships that brought the motor component parts were the source of the mags, and as soon as a fresh supply would hit the wharf, the word would spread and thus would begin the mad scramble for the mags. The ritual was always the same – the mags would be placed inside a brown folder – and those high up in the pecking order would have first read. One of my workmates in Industrial Relations was passing an office in the main building and saw one of the boys fetching the coveted brown folder. He rushed in and demanded the next reading – at twelve o'clock on the dot my mate was in possession of the prized folder.

"Hold the fort; suspend all phone calls for the next hour."

He shouted out instructions.

He shot off to the 'Jacks' with the brown folder stuffed inside his jacket; found himself a nice quiet cubicle, took his seat on the throne and tingling with anticipation proceeded to open the folder.

What a shock!

The folder contained the Wimpy Menu.

The young guys were forever playing tricks especially with the girls in the office. It was the age of the mini-skirt and the Ford girls embraced it to a ridiculous degree. Though it was never said, there seemed to be a competition amongst the younger females to see who would wear the shortest skirt; much to the horror of the more sedate female members of the staff.

"Did you see her skirt this morning; my God the belt was bigger than the dress?"

The arrival of a blonde bombshell one Monday morning lifted the stakes to monumental heights.   No wonder she was instantly christened 'Mortal Sin'.

She wore a micro – mini over magnificent legs and a see-through low cut top – she was out to crush the opposition into the ground. If that wasn't enough, she told one of the lads on her first day at work, that she couldn't be bothered wearing any panties on hot days; this fuelled the red-hot passions of the guys even more. The news that 'Mortal Sin' had been hired now spread to the factory floor, and fellows who had never been inside the office precinct in their lives, were now parading up the aisle of the main office to catch a glimpse of her ladyship in the typing pool.

'Mortal Sin' soon became an enigmatic type of character; firstly she stayed very much to herself while still flashing the equipment at every available moment in the typing pool. Though propositioned by many guys in the company she refused point blank to have anything to do with the Ford people – she did not believe in mixing work with social life. The mystery surrounding her deepened when someone discovered that she did not socialise at all; after work each evening she stayed at home and just looked at television. But she must have got great satisfaction from being the centre of attention – when she first joined the company she always entered the factory by the rear entrance, very soon afterwards she proceeded to walk through the factory; head erect, chest pushed forward, mini-skirt riding up her thighs, much to the amusement of the factory floor workers. As cool as a cucumber, she ignored the wolf-whistles and comments and preceded the couple of hundred yards journey to the main office, never batting an eyelid. One afternoon as she was making her way through the factory in the usual manner the noise was at fever pitch when suddenly a scratchy Cork voice was heard over the entire din:

"Charlie," the voice rang out across the entire length of the body shop,

"Would you ride 'Mortal Sin'?"

"Ride her," came the reply, "I'd ride the fellow that rode her."

The noise level hit a new high, and reverberated throughout the whole factory as the other departments took up banging on the metal frames of the cars. Car assembly plants are synonymous with boredom, and "Mortal Sin" did her bit to lift the doom and gloom of that factory.

If sex was high on the agenda in Fords, so also was snobbery and; the quintessential exponent was a man known as 'The Den'. He had a dapper appearance and roamed the offices and factory apparently immune to all and sundry. No one knew much about him, only that he had come from England some twenty years before; he was given a plum job, a big salary and fuck-all work to do. Rumours persisted that he was promised the MD job, and when it never materialised he got on his high horse and refused to have anything to do with the peasant Irish. One afternoon there was unbelievable commotion in the main office; apparently a cat got stuck behind the partition and our hero The Den came to the scene. Seeing the plight of the old cat The Den immediately swung into action. He went out into the factory; picked up a lump hammer, returned to the scene of the cat and proceeded to demolish the entire wall. He picked up the cat and shagged off leaving the entire mess behind. After that episode he went up two notches in my book.

It is difficult, at this remove, to understand the influence Fords had in Ireland at the time. In Cork alone, they had a very large workforce and a couple of hundred pensioners, and this resulted in millions of pounds pouring into the Cork economy each week. Ford employees were paid about twice the national average which was a great boon to the city. Fords carried power, and this was evident in the manner the banks treated Ford personnel, particularly if they thought they carried some weight within the company. When The Den entered the bank they almost lit a candle, but the old boy treated them with the same disdain that he treated everyone else. One day, while he was conducting some business with the company bankers; of course the assistant manager was serving him; he asked to cash a personal cheque. While the Assistant Manager was counting out the money he put his thumb into his mouth to make it easier to count the money. When the counting was finished The Den just stood there and made no attempt to take his money. When the Assistant Manager asked if everything was OK; The Den replied

"Could I have some dry notes please?"

This guy could have been killed any day, but he survived, and a few years later I retired him from the company. Strange to say, as a pensioner, I had a lot of contact with him, and we became quite friendly. It seemed to me that he was bitter towards Fords, and he certainly detested the Irish, and never went out of his way to hide that fact. They say if you spit in the wind in Kerry you would hit a writer or a poet, and the same could be said about extraordinary characters in Fords. The Den was a prominent eccentric, but we had our home grown as well. One of these characters was a footballer, sort-of, before he moved into the 'player manager' code. He was built like a brick shit-house, and when he would park himself in front of the goal, you would need a ton of semtex to move him out of there. But like all shit-houses he got old, and his old pins started to give him trouble, which forced him to employ other tactics – like knocking guys out with his fists. But the referees started to hand him out red cards as if it was Christmas, and as he was now too old to start a career in the ring, he decided to go into full-time coaching with Fords. You could say he was fond of a pint, and his after-training binges were something to behold.

The team was playing a tournament away from home, and the bold coach approached the management for funds to participate. His request for funding was generously granted and off they went with bulging wallets and great expectations.

However their exit from the competition was both swift and unexpected, so they headed for the boozer to drown their sorrows. Five hours later they were still drowning their sorrows, but the wallet was still bulging. Hard as they tried, they were unable to spend the kitty and did not like the idea of handing back any cash to the company. The coach took decisive action – he went out to the back on the pub, stuck his finger down his throat and vomited up a few gallons of porter, went back into the pub and called for more drink until the kitty was well and truly spent.

But another man who never took a drink could have been Cork's own Basil Fawlty – he was a foot shorter, two stone heavier, performed the same mad antics, was more loquacious and was home grown. He was responsible for the food in Fords, in other words he was laughingly titled, The Catering Manager. When I first joined Fords I was advised that the soup in the canteen was no good at all until Friday; but due to my youth and naivety it did not register with me. However after a few weeks on the job and picking up the odd comment flying about that one could trot a mouse over the soup on Fridays; the penny finally dropped.

Basil or Flintstone as we knew him ruled over the canteen like a latter-day dictator; somehow he always carried the expectancy that things would go wrong.

And was he right there!

The menus for the canteen could have been written in stone and cemented into the ground, because there was no danger in the world that they would ever be changed. Spring came and summer, and the autumn leaves signalled the arrival of winter but the menus remained the same. Some employees could only tell the day of the week by the menu posted on the walls of the factory. I learned from bitter experience that the one thing you didn't do in Fords was to criticise the food. Flintstone simply went ballistic. I had the stupidity to say to him one day that I thought that there was a strange taste from the beef. His face reddened to boiling point, his eyes bulged like the eyes of a trapped pike, and he moved both hands Moses-like and opened his mouth but no sound came out. Like the televisions of the sixties we had a picture and no sound. When his voice box eventually made contact with his mouth, he roared about the place in an incoherent manner.

"What the fuck do you know about beef, I've been in this business all my life and I never put a bad meal in front of anyone?"

"Listen, I said, I'm not making any accusations, and I'm just merely telling you what I have noticed."

By this stage the sweat was gathering on his forehead and trickling down the channels on his face. I decided to back off in case he was about to suffer some serious injury in front of me, and I could be held responsible.

"I was probably wrong," I said,

And without further ado scurried back to my office. Just as I was about to leave for home that evening, who is coming towards me but the bold Flintstone himself.

"I think I went over the top today, look takes these few steaks with you, it will help to heal the rift."

This was the other side of Flintstone – a lovable rogue on occasions.

In the sixties there was more segregation in Fords than there was in South Africa.

There were three canteens: one for the hourly paid employees – the assembly operatives, the second for the office staff and the third for the Hob Knobs – directors and managers. The food also fell into the three categories in reverse order – bad, worse and disaster. I dined under the banner of worse.

We had a crotchety old guy dining with us who was about two months away from retirement, and he insisted that chops be served to him every day, for he did not like the fare on offer – quel surprise! Flintstone had made a mighty concession for him in providing this a la carte option – chops. One day Flintstone served the chops himself and assumed an attitude as if he was doing our friend a great favour. When Flintstone returned later and asked if he enjoyed the chops he was savaged by the cranky little man.

"Don't ask me if I enjoyed those shaggin chops – Christ, you must have cut them with a razor blade."

So guess what happened the next day – Cranky had half a lamb served up to him on his plate. Flintstone had the great ability to put down minor insurrections instantly.

On another occasion when a girl complained that there were two hairs in her dinner; all hell nearly broke out with the restaurant staff and of course Flintstone was sent for – he quickly dragged his fleshy body to the scene of the crime. The girl was furious.

"Look, there are two hairs in my dinner – this is scandalous."

Flintstone crouched down to examine the plate. After a thorough examination, Flintstone lifted himself to his full five foot four inches, and with a glint in his eye, announced in a loud voice that there were not two hairs in her dinner – there was only one hair and it was sticking out in two places. Thus Flintstone lived his life, going around putting out little fires with humour and sometimes anger, fires that might grow into something bigger if they were left unattended.

In spite of the grub in the canteen many of the lads in the office were putting on the few pounds, especially the guys in their late thirties. Most of them had bid farewell to sport and all forms of exercising when they hit the magical thirty mark, as was the norm in those far-off days. So in one of the more creative periods in the office, one of the crew suggested that we run a diet competition – and about twenty signed up for the challenge. We were well aware of the mathematical advantage that a real roly-poly guy would have over the field in a first past the post system, but we all agreed that percentages were not our strong points, so whoever lost the most weight between weighing-in day and weighing-out day would capture the loot. The weighing–in day was reminiscent of the heavyweight championship of the world but with much more noise and excitement, as fellows pulled every ruse to weigh heavier. Pockets full of coins, thick army-styled boots and heavy waistcoats were employed to deceive the scrutinizers. Eventually after much argument and hullabaloo the weighing was completed and recorded in the black book and the fun began.

And the moaning …

"I'm fucking starved I'd eat a scabby child."

"My stomach is gone in so much you could play the Boys of Kilmichael on my ribs."

And so the days drew on.

The competition was due to last two weeks but within a short few days there was already an anti-post favourite emerging. Pat had taken a few lengths out of the field, and if he could hold his advantage he would be clear by the end of the week. But the weekends were notorious for him to keep out of the boozer and the chip shops of Cork. He was once quoted as saying that no red-blooded breathing human being with a few pints of porter on board could pass a chipper on his way home from the pub. So we waited, with baiter breathe, to see how the favourite would handle the weekend – the pot of money was a big incentive if he could only keep the feedbag away from the mouth. Monday morning saw the chirpy favourite at his desk and his smile would indicate that he was well down on the scales. Some of his close competitors had already given up the ghost – the best way to get rid of temptation is to give in to it. By the weigh-in, our favourite had stretched further away and won by a country mile – total weight loss amounted to nineteen pounds. To celebrate the competition, as distinct from loss of weight, the group decided to go away for the weekend to Youghal. When our favourite returned on Monday morning we decided to give him another weigh-in as the scales was still hanging around, and low and behold he had gained back the entire nineteen pounds and another four for good measure.

Another piece of madness occurred when Leevale Athletic Club were making an attempt on the world twenty-four hour relay in Wilton. The chairman of the club rang me at Fords and asked me if I could organise to have The Lord Mayor of Cork start the relay on the Saturday. The Mayor was well known to me so I rang him in City Hall and he was delighted to do it. I had arranged to pick him up on the day and to take him to the venue to start the proceedings. I got the feeling when I picked him up that he had a smell of drink on his breath and as we were passing up Western Road he asked me to stop the car and go in for one drink. Christ one drink is right. He had two or three pints followed by three chasers in the space of an hour – I was frantic to get him out to the venue, and I was in some state to get him to the start on time. Because it was an attempt on the world record the whole thing had to run bang on time. Eventually I managed to get him outside the door of the pub but I noticed that his feet were buckling, his Mayoral Chain was swinging round his neck and his voice had died in his throat, so I loaded him into the car and made haste for the venue. When the assembled masses saw the Mayor emerging from the car they burst into instant applause to welcome him – he waved to acknowledge their acclamation – and walked straight as a dye into the tent behind the start. Jez, I thought, the viper has sobered up in the space of fifteen minutes. But it did not last long – for no sooner had he hit the tent than he was once more attacking the brandy bottle, which was on standby for the visiting dignitaries. When the time arrived to start the relay race, he was ushered to the start line; he put the gun over his head like Kit Carson, fired once in the air, and headed straight back into the for more brandy. It took a gross lie to get him to leave – we had run out of drink – and I again ferried him to the City Hall and poured him back into his Mayoral Office.

Drink played as big a part in the lives of the people in the seventies as it does today.

On one occasion 'The Braz' – a piano player of some note and myself were invited to Dublin by the Player Wills Company as recognition for the originality of the script that I had written for the Tops of the Town show with Fords. We joined in, on a music session in the bar, with The Dubliners and we were chucking it out with Luke and the boys. There was a free bar for the invitees and during the evening a couple of women of the night had wormed their way into the private function and had parked themselves at the counter and availed of the free booze. They must have imbibed some drink, for when two of them were going to the bathroom they walked straight through a glass door, shattering it into a thousand pieces. The sing-song came to an abrupt end as the two were carted off to the accident and emergency.

And our mighty music session was finished for the night.

Those crazy happenings and events at Ford seem a million miles away now – we were young and crazy and willing to grab the world by the arse, who could have thought then that we would ever grow old and be crotchety little bastards, but alas it happened.

CHAPTER SIX

When I awoke on my fiftieth birthday I wished I had died on my fortieth.

Forget the lark about not dying a young man – I was living in a kind of limbo trying to live up to the expectations the insurance company had bestowed on me – House Husband. My household chores all attained the same importance in my life – walking the dog, cleaning the oven, putting the bin out on Thursday morning, washing the fecking bin, running for the occasional bottle on milk or a sliced pan, preparing the rustic stew and chasing codgers and chancers from the front door.

I needed to escape!

But just when I thought that my life could not descend any further and that by now I had exhausted the medical lexicon, along comes another intruder like a thief in the night.

Eye migraine if you don't mind.

It hit me like a southern tornado right out of the blue. I can seriously say that in all my years of existence on this planet I had never heard of a single person who suffered from that condition. But somehow, someone up there thought that I was an appropriate candidate.

It first hit me in the gym, which I had joined to get myself out of the house.

Anyone who ever possessed a black and white telly in the sixties will understand what eye migraine is like – squiggly lines jumping incessantly across your eyes just like the telly in Ireland in its infancy. Another hurdle to be overcome – another jump for me. But like every other misfortune that was flung at me, I had to get myself into the right state of mind to overcome it.

And the gym was a big help to me in diverting the attention away from it.

If I am not mistaken it was one of the English Sunday newspapers that had a motto that told us "that all human life was there".

Believe me in the gym I found it.

It is no wonder in the wide world that I contracted such a disease as eye migraine – the sights on show would cause all sorts of disturbances to anyone's nervous system. Starting with myself – I had now blossomed into the complete Sumo wrestler. I had everything – the thick neck, the bald head with the tiny patch of hair, the big belly stretching out around me like a fleshy tutu, and the bulky legs completed the profile.

Is it any wonder that I found myself surrounded by homosapiens!

It was the female of the species that first got my undivided attention. She was a tall angular woman, straight as a flagpole, and she walked sideways round the gym and swimming pool area. As a young lad in Cork I had encountered a man who had the misfortune to have a disease in his back, which meant that he was permanently bent over backwards. But by some miracle he defied the laws of gravity; somehow he found his way round the city much to the hilarity of the youngsters who followed him around and taunted him with the name of "Johnny Look Up In The Sky".

While poor Johnny had a medical condition, the lady in the gym was just a nutter. This was not a permanent affliction she possessed, not by a long mile. One day I saw her on the treadmill walking as straight as a dye. But she was not a one-trick pony – not the Angular Woman. On this particular morning I was about to subject my body to the rigours of the steam room, so I duly removed my prescription goggles – thereby reducing the whole world to a haze. I slowly entered the steam room. The sight that confronted my eyes caused me to immediately throw back on the goggles. There she was – the Angular Woman – her legs spread-eagled and a foot on each bench, her hands stretching up to the ceiling and the steam rising up around The Gap of Dunloe. It was a frightening sight for any man to behold, especially to a man of my delicate disposition. Without moving a muscle, but just sensing me in the background she calmly informed me that this was great exercise for the posture. I totally agreed and quickly beat a hasty retreat least some other geezer would find their way into the stream room and find me leering at The Angular Woman. I could be ruined for life. Coming out of the steam room with the goggles still in situ, I must have presented an odd figure to the other inmates of this particular Zoo, so without further ado I headed straight for the pool.

I was in such a hurry to get out of eyeshot that I dragged my seventeen stone torso through the water as if I were Mark Spitz. Perhaps the onlookers might have thought that I looked like a retreating sperm whale. Strange at it may seem but most of the inmates got used to the antics of The Angular Woman, and she became less a topic of conversion in the coming weeks. Perhaps it's because we had an influx of other nut cases in the interim.

The most obvious of the eccentrics was a fat man who came decked out with two rings piercing his nipples. These were not your ordinary old common rings that you would see on the average stud; no these were two large gold rings, and to my untrained eye would appear to be the Real McCoy – the full twenty-four carat. Believe me when I tell you, that these rings were so big that I would say that if he was harnessed properly he could pull a trap round the city without too much difficulty. But it was in the dressing area that he showed his true colours. Having divested himself of his last piece of apparel, he then proceeded to parade round in his birthday suit, displaying a large medallion dangling from his retributory cudgel, much to the merriment of the onlookers. Now whether this was a permanent fixture was not ascertained by the voyeurs, but all agreed afterwards, when our Stud disappeared, that it was hell of a cargo for any man to carry around – even for a man of his immense bulk. When he continued to dangle his medal in the paddock it became clear to the beady-eyed among us that he was only using his do-da for purely plumbing duties. One inmate suggested that if he were given it on a plate he would run a mile.

You can't fool all the inmates all the time!

Just when the antics of The Stud were becoming routine he pulled another stunt out of the top drawer. My goggles nearly steamed up again in the paddock area, when in addition to his dangling medal, he was now sporting two large and colourful butterflies on the cheeks of his arse. This guy was determined to stay in the limelight. And he did for a while; but such is the fickleness of man that very quickly the new kid on the block – the one-legged treadmill walker, stole his clothes. When I first caught sight of him I was sure the eye migraine was acting up again. One-legged man on a treadmill – now wouldn't that make you feel guilty!

He achieved this great feat by using his crutches to get to the treadmill, then he would lever himself onto the apparatus, and when his hands were fully secured on both handles off he went – well in a metaphorical sense. Over the weeks he built a fair old pace – enough to send the beads of sweat swirling down the crevices of his craggy face. We were all filled with admiration for him and he gave me the little fillip if not ambition to do better and try and bring the Sumo Body into some semblance of normality.

"With my dying breath, may I be able to say I'll start again."

This was all I needed.

I forced myself to look at the long mirror. The man inside looked back accusingly.

"Christ, do you know what I need … a toupee."

Eureka!

Yes, that would be the business!

This, coupled with my new gym regime, could recreate a new me.

I donned an old cap, put it arse-ways round on my head and gazed at the new spectacle. With the bare head covered, I must say I did not look a day over fifty, and maybe, just maybe, if it was hair that was covering the patch I might not look a day over forty. I could feel the excitement rising in my veins and coasting round my body. Without mentioning anything to the wife I hotfooted it down to the credit union the following morning. I decided to hit them for two grand – going for the Rolls Royce of toupees or nothing at all. No man on the planet would put down 'toupee' into the 'reason for loan column' and I was not going to be the odd man out. I decided to go the full hog and tell them that I was going to Cork to look after a dying relative. That would surely seal the deal and if it required a tear or two to copper fasten the loan that could be provided as well. I need not have worried. In ten minutes I had the cheque tightly gripped in my sweaty little paw and heading for the bank. Not a word to a single soul until I was fully decked out with my new toupee.

For a man of my years I spent an inordinate amount of time in front of the mirror when the coast was clear. I examined the lines on my face, the colour of my skin, the turn-up on my nose and every other minute detail that might influence the magical purchase that was about to adorn my head in the coming weeks. Whatever else might go wrong, my research would not be the reason for any failure. I toyed with the idea of buying over the Internet – in this way I could be fully assured that my anonymity would not be jeopardised. But with security the way it is in this weary world, it would more than likely be examined and pulled asunder by the customs people, while searching for explosives or drugs. And in addition, I would not like my hair to be peeping through a parcel as it was being delivered to my house – the neighbours might think I'm running a business in exotic animals. For all those logical reasons I decided to do my little bit of business on home-soil.

I scanned the golden pages until I found an agency with an unpronounceable foreign name – in this way I could be certain that no neighbour, friend or acquaintance would have any connection with my family or me. I made that phone call – a girl with broken English answered it. Could not be more perfect! I made the appointment and pointed out to the girl that I was a man of shy disposition and that confidentiality was my top priority. Having being assured I whistled away from the phone and pondered on the new me; breezing into the gym, my gear bag slung casually over my shoulder, my isotonic drink at the ready and the scantily clad model-types eyeing me up as if I was the new Cillian Murphy.

My wife noted my particular good form as we watched the telly that night and remarked that all the medication was doing some good at long last. I agreed, least I let the cat out of the bag. Having being bald since my early twenties I could not remember a time in my adult life when I possessed a head of hair. Next Wednesday my life would change forever.

The great day arrived. I threw on the new black suit, the crispy white shirt and the red and white Baptist tie and off with me with a spring in my step and a song on my lips. The day could not have gone better. I completed my business with the secrecy of a Free Mason and everything was scheduled for a fitting in two weeks.

But the man who invented toupees invented disasters.

I duly arrived for my fitting on the appointed day, and when the glue-like substance was administered to my head, and the hair firmly in place I left the building hoping to face the world with a new impetus.

This was my time to make an impression on the world!

When I arrived home, the wife took one look at me and she broke down. Inconsolable is the only word that comes to mind – she threatened instant divorce. She cried first, and then flew into a rage and roared at me so much that she woke the dog from his slumbers, and he instantly attacked me thinking I was some kind of intruder.

I was distraught.

In one mighty effort to prize the toupee from my head I pulled so hard that I lifted o a piece of my scalp with the offending object, and the blood gushed forth and ran down my face. With all the mayhem going on I did not realise that the dog had drawn blood as well, and it was now pouring out of my leg. The offending toupee was strewn on the white carpet like a dying rat trying to escape; the blood was oozing out of me by the bucket-load and the carpet was changing colour to a crimson red by the second.

When I woke up a Filipino nurse was rubbing my brow and Tallaght Hospital. The wife was standing nearby and, when I looked in her direction, she stared back with the calmly informing me that I was securely ensconced in the Accident and Emergency in disappointed look that I had woken up at all. I needed blood and a bed, and a good kick in the arse for being such a gobshite. My body went into another paroxysm when I remembered that the wife was still unaware of the two grand loan from the credit union.

Where can you find a gun or rope when you need one!

But the sun goes down even on the roughest day, and soon I was back in the homestead – but this time quieter than the proverbial church mouse. As the days passed by, and some things were attaining a sense of normality, I became philosophical and decreed that whatever hair the Good God had allocated for my head would be OK by me, and never would I tamper with nature again.

I had learned a harsh lesson.

Wasn't he the very wise man who stated that sometimes we are as different from ourselves as we are from other people. My vainglorious act had brought me down a cul-de-sac where, in addition to almost wrecking my marriage, I almost lost my life.

When you have a beaten hand it takes a man to admit it and move on. So when the bandages were removed, and the blood count looked somewhat respectable for a man of my age and state of health, I made my return to the gym. With my ego still in need of repair, and my wounds almost healed, my return was turning out to be very therapeutic. The angular woman was now walking backwards all the time in and out of water without the slightest notice being taken of her. There was a new influx of women who had their best athletic days behind them. Much to the annoyance of the serious swimmers – including moi – these women would gather in the pool and create a large circle nattering and laughing among themselves and blocking pool traffic without the slightest embarrassment. In fact one could say that they were totally unaware of anyone else in the pool. They were known by all and sundry as the BOTTS (broads over the top). One morning, as the hot water was pelting my ample frame, I looked in the direction of the pool and the sight that assaulted my eyes caused me to think for a moment that the Lock Ness monster was over from Scotland on his summer vacation. I quickly retrieved my prescription goggles from my head and secured them to give me a better view of the pool. Three of the Botts had broken from the main school and were swimming one behind the other just like a line of signets; they were wearing inflatable wings and rising up and down in the water. This sight was worth the yearly membership itself. The BOTTS continued to set up camp in the middle of the pool, which caused the old fellows to mutter strings of personal insults under their breaths, as they dragged their weary limbs through the water. With old age taking firm control of the pool, the young females of the species were forced into parading round the perimeter of the pool displaying their equipment like displaced Hens.

I got displaced myself – this time in the steam room.

Sandwiched between Podge and Rodge.

Podge sat to my right and had a cough so dry and so sharp that one could swear that he was personally delivered to the gym by ambulance from the nearest TB sanatorium. Rodge had a guttural cough, wet and persistent and had the good manners to always cough in your face. I almost broke my leg escaping from the semi-darkness least I end up in the city morgue.   As a marked contrast to the weary and the dying that infested this joint, there was also a cohort of the very fit and able males – I would call them the belt and resin brigade. This particular branch of the species could be seen mostly in the gym lumping weights and applying this white powder to their hands by the bucket load. In the paddock these Adonis's were easily discernible by their rippling muscles, and their all-over tans and their attitude to the unfortunates like me.

How can a man with a full stomach understand a man with an empty stomach? Not a shaggin chance in the world.

One of the Unfortunates made the comment that they would not like to be in the trenches at the Battle of the Somme with some of those muscle men, but that statement was born of envy. The other Unfortunates like me had more pressing things on their minds like doing their utmost to stay over ground, and endeavouring to keep off the path that leads to the everlasting bonfire. The Unfortunates had their own unwritten hierarchical structure. While someone with the list of medical problems, such as myself, might feel near the summit, it became clear to me that I was further down the chain when I saw some of the new recruits that were beginning to populate this arena. We know about old friends –The Angular Woman, The One-Legged Treadmill Walker but they paled into insignificance when the paraplegic weightlifter arrived followed by the blind marathon woman. Seeing them overcoming such incredible odds day after day, and still maintaining a smile, made the rest of the Unfortunates stand back and admire. It put me in mind of a relative of my mother who visited us when we were young children. To be honest she frightened the be-Jesus out of us with her funny speech, her humpy back and mad antics. She gesticulated to all and sundry, and when she attempted to speak she spat at everyone and everything within eyeball distance. She never left home without a flash lamp, and believe me she provided a terrifying spectacle to the children as she wormed her way round the city at night. She was known to all as Deaf Annie and her story was widely known, thanks to my own mother. When Annie was about four years old she contracted diphtheria, which resulted in her losing her speech. But by some quirk of nature all the words she had learned up to her illness stayed in her head. This was her vocal lexicon for life, and all her speech and mutterings came from the one tiny vocabulary. But she had an ingenious brain for getting her message across. One night while we were sitting round the fire with Deaf Annie in our midst, she was pointing out to my father that she met this man in England called, "Tommy the Iron".

My father and mother were totally flummoxed.

"Tommy the Iron" she kept repeating.

By this stage she was spitting on us kids like the local fire brigade putting out a blaze, for she was totally frustrated that no one understood her. Eventually she pulled a piece of paper and biro from her bag and proceeded to write.

"Tommy the Iron" turned out to be "Tommy Steel".

We laughed. She laughed until she fell backwards off the chair. She was remarkable in the sense that nothing ever got the better of her. This was the kind of unquenchable spirit we saw in the gym, and some of the Unfortunates including myself did see how well off we were, and in spite of everything we did take time out to smell the roses.

But being over fifty has all the drawbacks and none of the advantages, especially if one is operating as a House Husband. The mood can change with the blink of an eye. The gym was losing its lustre, especially when it was failing in its primary task of reducing my carcass to appropriate proportions.

When I first set foot in the gym I looked forward as a child might look forward to Christmas, to immersing my body in the scalding waters of the Jacuzzi. But now the entire business of stripping off my cloths, and throwing on the bathing trunks became a laborious exercise. Somehow the pool, once healer on my creaking frame, was no longer attractive. There was a mood swing in me beginning at my shoelaces and reaching the top of my skull, so much so that I began to write my poems again. And every poem around that time reflected a lonesome man looking at the world with a jaundiced eye.

The Unfortunates didn't know what to make of me when I began to recite these poems to them in the paddock, but the general in the gym consensus was that something had snapped inside my cranium and that I should give up reciting poetry lest the entire group be pulled ashore by the men in white coats. The Crosswords Man said it was the approach of the Male Menopause that was to blame for my strange behaviour, and that it was a well-documented fact, that it was as severe and destructive to the male as it was to the female of the species. Before he goes near a doctor, said old Charlie with the stutter, I would like to take him on hand. It was a well-known fact that Charlie dabbled in alternative medicine. He once told me that he started his medical career when he first discovered Ginseng in the late sixties and since then has had more cures to his name than Padre Pio. Of course he had long since graduated from Ginseng – he had the full Chinese Medicine Take-Away Menu at his disposal, and he surely had the cure for a man with a problem like mine.

At this stage in my life I was so depressed I was tuning into Radio Na Gaeltachta on a regular basis, and as you might imagine the family had relinquished all hope of me returning to Terra Firma again. Desperate events call for desperate measures so I embraced Charlie's Chinese medicine. One day and out of sight of the patrons of the paddock, he produced a potion which I downed in one gulp. Christ it was ten times worse than cabbage water I had used on my diet. I resisted with all my being the strong temptation to throw up, and empty the contents of my stomach into the used towel bin. I contorted my face like a Kerryman who had just lost the All-Ireland final, and placed both hands on the pit of my stomach. The heat emanating from that region of my anatomy was approaching boiling point. And me, unable to contain myself any longer, cried out to high heavens.

This brought a posse of attendants and fitness instructors scurrying to my side.

"Jesus, I'm fucking poisoned; the bastard is after poisoning me. I'm poisoned," I continued to cry out; "the stuttering little fucker has poisoned me."

By this stage, Charlie thinking that I was on death's doorstep shot out the emergency exit, and disappeared into the traffic. Meanwhile the attendants were endeavoring to get me to the first aid room. I had a gusher in transit – the sick shot from my mouth into the air only for it to dive straight into the pool. This caused more confusion than the dropping of the atomic bomb in Nagasaki. The swimmers in the pool were scattering left, right and centre – trying frantically to evacuate the scene. The Botts in the centre of the pool were still totally unaware of the impending disaster and continued to laugh and mutter among themselves. By now, as if by some magic I seemed to be back to normal health – the pain well and truly gone!

All the bile and poison from my stomach was now deposited in the pool, and I felt wonderful. When I related my story to the attendants, how Charlie had administered the medicine to me, they immediately sent the security into the street in hot pursuit of the Chinese Miracle Man, but they were unable to find a single trace of his whereabouts. He returned two weeks later to the scene of the crime disguised under a hat, and sporting a fuzzy beard. He brought along a doctor's note saying he was unwell and would not be in a position to maintain his membership, and therefore would be seeking a refund of his fee. When the attendants got wind that he was on the premises, he was frog-marched to the front door and told in no uncertain manner to take himself and his Hippocratic Oath to another location.

In retrospect, I felt Charlie was badly treated. After my episode in the gym I felt much better and in the coming days I went from strength-to-strength.

Charlie had performed the miracle.

And the Menopause was never mentioned again.

Soon things returned to abnormality in the gym and my little incident boosted my standing in the paddock. One abnormality that was rearing its head was the behavior of the BOTTS – they seemed to be walking sideways in the pool whenever they broke from the main school. Christ, I thought, they must have picked up this disease from The Angular Woman – I was totally unaware that strange behavior was a contagious disease, and maybe should be reported to the World Health Organization. This could turn out to be more deadly than Bird Flu or cause more destruction than The Black Plague. But I had caused enough trouble so I held my whist and left it to others. Keep your head down and your mouth closed especially when near the swimming pool.

I had discovered a new mantra!

CHAPTER SEVEN

With my star in the ascendancy once more, the woman down at the Social Welfare Office thought it might be a good career move for me to get some IT training, so without further ado, I enrolled with FÁS there and then. I was feeling real perky as you can imagine changing my title from House Husband to FÁS Trainee –

"You've come up in the world and it's all to your credit."

I just hummed to myself as I made my way home.

I did not envy FÁS their work endeavoring to get information into a hardened thick skull like mine. When I was finally called for training I nervously joined the group of trainees. I was like a child in the confirmation class waiting for the catechism examination by the Bishop. My classmates were all women mostly in their twenties and thirties, and while other men might view this as an opportunity from heaven, I saw it as a potential risk to life and limb for a man of my delicate health. We all know about the hazards of spending six hours a day peering at a computer screen, but it is an entirely different matter looking at the bare thighs of young women from morning to evening. But I need not have worried – the biggest lump of a woman this side of the equator, complete with army fatigues, placed herself right in front of me, and not only did she block the view of the ladies, she blocked the light from the sun. I was like a man living in the foothills on the Andes. Behind me sat The Pointy Woman who repeated everything the instructor said, as if she was permanently switched on to repetitive mode. Although this class was in its infancy, I quickly realised that my patience could be severely tested.   Everything about the Pointy woman seemed to finish at a point – face, hands and especially her nose. If she possessed the dexterity I have no doubt she would be able to pull a thorn from any arse such was the pointiness of her nose. Our class spent the first hour learning to turn the bloody computer on and off, but as I was conversant with the WP technology due to the fact that my wife had bought me machine years back – I was a dab hand.

Just into the second hour of the lesson I was glad to see the appearance of another male trainee (hardly in the first flush of youth) who was introduced to the group.

He could have come straight from the nearest funeral home, his face ashen colour under his cap which was still plonked on his head. His nose was a deep red and looked as if it had ambitions to expand and fill his face and he had frightened eyes plunked inside a massive skull.

"This is Mickey," said the instructor, "he has come to join our happy little group."

At least now I was not the only man on the island.

By the time we got down to our first real lesson it was time for lunch. On the first strike of the clock at one, the girls scattered as if the building was going up in smoke, leaving myself and Mickey stranded like two beached whales caught out by the tide. As a man in possession of an elongated face myself (a baldy devil) I am sympathetic to any old geezer who is a bit scarce on top, but one thing I cannot tolerate is the man in denial.

And Mickey appeared to be that man.

For the entire class Mickey never made an attempt to remove the cap from his head, even when prompted to do so by the instructor, and when the break came he was glad to inform the instructor that he would prefer to keep the cap in place during classes.

"Haven't got much on top," is how he put it.

And you haven't much hair either I whispered under my breath.

But I held my whist as I did not want to drive the only male, other than myself, into Limbo. When we assembled at two I tried to extradite myself from the proximity of the menace by changing seats, but The Pointy Woman had my every move covered and gesticulated to all and sundry that I had returned to a different seat. I bowed to the old bag – coward as I am, and crawled back to my original seat cursing the old hag under my breath.

"It would be best if we all maintained the same seating arrangements," said the instructor. The Pointy Woman was smiling like the Cheshire cat.

And she, having consumed the father and mother of a subsidized lunch, was ready for more action – in a manner of speaking. For no sooner had we all settled down in front of our screens when up comes the volume – herself was snoring to high heaven. The instructor possessed all the courage of an Italian General, and he flatly refused to wake her from her slumbers as the class dragged on.

"She will wake in her own good time," he muttered.

By this stage I was half expecting Mickey to join the snoring chorus himself.

By the time "Herself" was fully awake we had arrived at Fonts – but without Mickey. He was still fumbling with the on/off switch.

It appeared at this juncture that Mickey would not light up the world with his computer skills, well this side of the grave at least. The instructor appeared to be a mild mannered man and even in the throes of showing Mickey how to start up the bloody computer he never lost the rag.

"You will get it eventually – keep practicing."

The instructor beat a hasty retreat from Mickey's desk and The Mature Student   returned to the intricacies of the on/off button.

But this world is a very unfair place. While Mickey was struggling big-time, young Mona was cruising ahead. She was absorbing information like the proverbial sponge and was forging ahead of the class. She was doing all this with a set of earphones firmly planted in her ears and a mobile phone at the ready on her desk. Her dexterity was something to behold as she did her computer tasks, listened to her music and sold semi-detached houses on her mobile phone all at the same time – all this without a murmur of protest from the instructor. He, like the rest of us, was so dumbfounded, he was paralyzed to intervene. And so the show dragged on.

I was comatose by four o clock from the constant attention I was giving the bloody computer and was quite dizzy when I hit the outside light. My old brain had been half dead for ages, and now, when I was forcing it to do some work, it revolted like a South American General. I bade farewell to the other inmates with the little bit of energy I had left, and wondered how in Gods name I was going to walk the half mile home. As I dragged my weary body along I understood with perfect clarity what it would be like to scale Mount Everest. I contemplated at one stage throwing myself on the footpath but I quickly dismissed that idea when I contemplated spending five hours in an A&E Department – that would surely finish me off! But the body wants to survive, even when the mind wants to call it a day, and therefore in spite of all the hardship, I survived to attend for another day ... and another day ... and another day!

Soon, I had completed a week and advanced to 'Copy and Paste'. By this stage the bold Mickey had progressed to touching and pressing the keys on the keyboard. Some of the girls were saying he might even be the worst IT student in Europe if not in the world. Women being women (they will never be like us) had formed themselves into little groups and at lunchtime would gravitate to their own section of the canteen discussing motherhood, nappy rash, potty training, George Clooney and so on, while Einstein (Mickey) and myself stared into our brown soup hardly uttering a word.

And so my life went on …

It was not the auspicious return to education I had envisioned, but I was doing OK on the course, and with Mickey not performing I felt the hand of history on my shoulder to defend the intelligence of the male. The days flowed by and tumbled into weeks, which meant we were facing into our first exam.

Microsoft Word.

Everyone seemed ready except of course our old comrade – he was moving at his own pace.

THE FIRST MODULE OF THE ECDL.

It was great for a geezer like me to get this opportunity to sit an exam at my now advancing years, and I was relishing the challenge. The room was mouse quiet as The Instructor handed out the paper…

Switch on the computer and away we go!!!

The calamity happened in the first ten minutes and the irony was not wasted on me, as I was on 'Mail Merging' at the time. Mickey had totally lost the plot by this stage and was hitting out at random keys to beat the band. All sorts of programmes and images were shooting up on the screen until it eventually crashed with the image of George Bush and Osama Bin Laden firmly fixed on the screen in a very compromising position. No matter what keys Mickey pressed he could not get the two off the screen. The women within eyeshot of Mickey's computer screen were inconsolable with laughter. The sweat poured from under Mickey's cap and trundled down onto his craggy face, and when he couldn't take anymore he leaped from his chair letting out an almighty squeak and headed for the door and was not seen again.

And I was the only man left on the island!

And my life was about to change. Change utterly.

I'm not sure whether it was Oscar or Bernard who said

'That all women should be married but not men'.

Whoever said it anyway, must have had firsthand knowledge of FÁS women.

Mickey had flown and a battalion of solders could not find him, so I was left at the mercy of this flock of women. Now that I was alone amongst women, the dynamic of the group changed. Bit-by-bit the women began to mother me – at the ten o'clock break it first became evident. Thick juicy slices of apple tart, cream doughnuts, chocolate log, yes and even thick gudges of porter cake were all placed before me.

I was lapping up the attention, never mind the grub, as if I were a world cup holder. But these women were relentless – the way to a fat man's heart is through his lunchbox – and by God they had learned that lesson. At lunchtime the females had split up into two distinct groups and I got the distinct impression that they were vying with each other as to who could feed me the most. I was the meat in the sandwich and what a piece of meat – seventeen stone and rising every day.

And I could not resist the temptation, never mind cutting back. I must have been eating half my weight in food each day, taking into consideration the massive amount of tasties supplied by the ladies of the class at tea break, the huge subsidized meal I ate at lunchtime, and then when I returned home I would have another crack at the dinner. I was bursting out of every stitch of clothing. My wife was doing Novenas during the evenings and consulting Anthony Robbins over the Internet during the day, in some vain effort to get me to stop eating, but I was like a juggernaut pounding down the motorway without any brakes. In my case, it was true that education was seriously damaging my health. But it was the custard pies of The Pointy Woman that brought me to my senses – she had baked them especially for me! Christ, I thought to myself, if she is getting in on the act it's time to have a fresh look at my life …

And I did not like the mutton-skulled individual that looked out at me from the long mirror. What started off as an adventure into the complicated and intriguing world of the computer was now turning out to be one of the biggest disasters of my life.

I had been down that boreen before, and fortunately had good experience of extraditing myself from self-inflicted mishaps and injuries. So as before, and just before I am whipped off the planet, it was back to the air shoes and the steady walk in the park, unfortunately the old dog had been worn out by now, so the wife ever loyal was my constant companion. I once again endeavored to shake off some of the mutton from my creaking old frame. As I began to lose the odd few pounds I could push my body into a forty-six trousers without the possibility of a button flying off and taking the eye out of someone. When the females of the species realised I was not taking the bait (cakes) any longer they quickly lost interest in me – all along I was an old fool – just a pawn in the power struggle. When I refused to play ball they turned to other games to keep themselves occupied. I had escaped their clutches and like Martin Luther King … I was free at last … free at last!

With my avoirdupois not occupying my consciousness every moment of the day it was easier to put my mind back on my training. And as happened before in my life, I got this mad rush of energy and power. I was moving myself up the ladder and hoping to be the best in the class. With the consent of the tutor I took up a new position in the class, well out of humanities reach – well The Pointy Woman – and from my new launching pad I laid out my stall to take this class by storm. I was like a man possessed; IT was like my new religion and I was boring the ass off everyone.

"Have you got PowerPoint?"

"Are you using Excel for doing your tax returns yet?"

And this was outside of the class.

I had so much enthusiasm within the class that the tutor was convinced that I was overmedicating and he referred me to the doctor on the campus. But before I ever got to see the doctor the bubble burst – swift and alarming. While attending to one of the exercises; suddenly the whole place began to spin. The computer screen began to come towards my face and retract almost instantly – until eventually I ended up in a great big heap on the ground. When I came round the entire clutch of females were surrounding me. The Pointy Woman was preaching to the classmates that I had taken a heart attack – she remembered her own father had the same symptoms and expression as me before he kicked the bucket. For the first time the instructor took control of the situation and reprimanded Herself for such insensitivity, and ordered the others back to work at their desks. They were shocked by his harsh voice and force of character – they never thought he had it in him.

"Let China sleep …"

He took complete control of the situation. He loosened my collar, laid me out in a comfortable position, went on the blower to call for help, and frightened the bejesus out of the women with an almighty roar when they were slow returning to their desks. Soon help arrived, and by this stage I had recovered enough to walk to a waiting car. Just before I entered the car I turned around to the instructor and asked him where he had got all the training for dealing with emergencies.

He smiled.

"SAS, spent ten years there."

He turned on his heels.

Well Holy Smoke beat that. Gentle guy my arse!

The driver wanted to take me to the A&E but I thought I had suffered enough for one day, and asked him to take me home. All the activity in the park, wearing out the air shoes, plus the intense effort I had put into the IT training had taken it out of me, and like most endeavors in my life looked like it too was going to end in failure. Lying in my bed that afternoon gave me ample time to ponder on the enigma that was the instructor and again the wise words of my grandmother came floating back.

"The one thing in life is never to underestimate anyone."

I had fallen into the trap.

It was rest that was required and plenty of it. At my age, and with my medical record, I would never become a leading light in the information technology field, and as my GP reminded me I had enough illness's to be going on with without creating more. So it was back to the scratcher for a week or two. The texts from the females were flooding in to me in my bed – the news about the instructor was out, and he had replaced George Clooney as the number one pinup boy. The fickleness of the female of the species is something to behold.

Soon I was ready to return to my classes. I wondered what the atmosphere would be like now that everything had changed – changed utterly. Pinup boy or no pinup boy what I saw reminded me that a terrible ugliness had been born.

The Pointy Woman had gone AWOL after getting a rollicking from Your Man.

The rest of the females were quiet as Poor Clare Nuns as they got on with their work, as The Instructor paraded up and down the class like a marauding Tiger.

The quiet voice had gone after the metamorphosis, to be replaced by a no-nonsense Barrack–type growl. The mask had truly slipped and he was fully into his true personality. We got through Microsoft Access as if we were learning the abacus, and soon we were heading into our final exam. But it was my fate never to finish the course and take my final examination. It happened on one of my famous walks with the wife by my side. I was attempting to walk up the hill in our local park when suddenly I ceased up like a broken down old banger ... the engine would not work anymore or rather my legs refused to carry me. I rested on the bench and started to rant and rave about those bloody Indian curries – but it was a little more serious than that – for I was unable to walk home.

After a barrage of tests I was booked into The Blackrock Clinic for an angiogram. Anyone who has ever undergone the experience of having an angiogram will tell you it is one of the strangest experiences you will ever face. It is like attending the movies – your own movie. For the uninitiated, it requires a cardiologist to insert an opening in the groin area and to push a camera on a wire up to the heart just like a chimney sweep. The great thing about this is that one is able to see, at all stages, what is happening. For many, looking at the outside body is horrific enough without the added thrill of being able to see inside. It is not for the faint hearted, but I did not find it frightening even though I am one of the biggest cowards on the planet. When my filming was complete, the groin door was closed and I was returned to my hospital bed complete with tea and toast to await the findings.

And just like on every other occasion when I awaited medical news, it was bad.

I needed a heart-bypass!

The cardiologist went on to point out that I had two blockages and the only solution was a heart by-pass. The string of funny lines that my friends would be throwing at me flashed through my head.

"What have you got in common with Cashel?"

"You both had by-passes."

Somehow I could not find them funny at this moment. My concentration and intensity had moved to another level – a place where flippancy had no place.

I had a wife and teenage son … and now to inform them.

The cardiologist disappeared out of the room and left me to my thoughts on that grey November day. We are born alone and must die alone and now I had to contemplate having this operation alone. When I spoke the word alone to myself it somehow captured the peculiar mood I was feeling at the time.

I passed on the news as cheerily as I could to my wife and son when they came to collect me from the hospital – of course everything will be OK.

The next day was the hardest day of my life. Having reassured the cardiologist's secretary that I was fine when she rang me, I settled down for a relaxing read.

The quietness of the house brought to mind the old Irish saying – Cionnas Na Reilige – The Quietude of the Grave.

My mind was all over the place. My old habit of pushing the past, the present and the future all into the one moment made me more confused and anxious. Several times during the day, I stood before the long mirror and imagined someone opening up my chest ...

Christ the idea nearly drove me bonkers. I was persecuting myself beyond all reason. The doctor said my chances of not making it would normally be two per cent but in my case, with my additional problems, my odds would be four per cent.

Straight answer to a straight question!

One chance in twenty five – you would take those odds in the lotto.

But I would be taking those odds with my life.

Somehow now, the idea of doing well and showing off in the IT class seemed so remote and irrelevant. The image of The Instructor doing his army bit was but a remote shadow, as the new reality kicked in with vigour and vengeance.

I thought of the clever guys who dreamt up The Maslow Theory and how quickly our needs and expectations change – I was living proof of its validity.

The wearisome day lingered on and I put up the brave front for the family when they returned in the evening. I downed a few cans of Beamish before I hit the sack in the hope that I might get some bit of sleep – but to no avail. The blackest of images haunted me throughout the night to such an extent that before morning I took myself into the front room and plonked myself in front of the telly in an effort to divert my thoughts. I was exhausted now, and wondered, how bad things would get after my first appointment with the surgeon. To be sure, there was a hell before me if all this continued.

But the darkest hour is just before dawn. From somewhere out in the great beyond, came a torrent of strength, and it surged through my body. The depression and exhaustion disappeared like a retreating tide before the avalanche, and I was left with a magnificent feeling of power and strength. I stood in front of the long mirror and gawked at my chest again – this time without a scintilla of fear.

Fuck me, I was winning!

CHAPTER EIGHT

Over the space of two days I had scaled the entire landscape of emotions, and was about to enter my limbo period – that period before the big day. I had to be a good boy and eat my greens, take as much fresh air as I could, and eat as little as possible and still have the strength to be able to stand up for most of the day. I had sorted out the cash for the job, and had set up my first appointment with the surgeon to whom I would entrust my life. I was positive for some reason of which there was no earthly reason; something that baffled my nearest and dearest. But I was in brilliant form and totally positive about the entire outcome.

Was it some sort of Divine intervention?

If I was a believer I would be happy to give that explanation and everything would be hunky dory. Close friends who know about my ego, would surmise that the reason I was on top of the world was because I was the center of attention now – a place I had always hankered after. But beware of this world especially if you are happy in your shoes, for this world possesses a backlash. This was first noticed by Brendan Behan in the sixties

"If they don't get you by the beard they'd get you by the balls"

And so it came to pass!

I woke up on the morning of my big appointment with the surgeon with the worst flu ever visited upon a human being. I turned over in the bed to inform my wife about my misery only to find out that she was worse than me. We could have been struck down with the

Black Plague. There was no escape; I had to try and make my way to the Blackrock Clinic as everything was in place for my surgery in February 2000 which was galloping up on me at an alarming rate. I slowly maneuvered my torso under the shower, scraped the hair from my face, threw on the good suit, said farewell to the wife and wished her every good luck in trying to stay alive, grabbed my car keys and joined the morning traffic snaking its way towards Blackrock, while I coughed and barked like a hardened hobo behind the wheel. I cursed to the high heavens the Power that placed such a tough burden on a poor innocent man like myself – a man who never harmed a soul in his entire life. The criminals swan through life, buy homes in the south of Spain, spends their leisurely time tanning their hides and nothing ever befalls them. The self–pity arena is a place I normally abhor, but somehow I could do nothing to prevent myself from straying into it. I was a sad sick man whose logic and sense of humour had dissipated in the morning traffic. After circumnavigating the Clinic three times in an effort to get a parking space, I felt as if I had been away in space – my head was spinning so much. When finally I found a parking space and reached my destination in the clinic I almost fell in the door, much to the consternation of the well-manicured receptionist.

"You must be Mr. Archer."

And she seeing the condition I was in

"let me get you something to drink."

"Make it a treble whiskey I spouted out, forgetting my surroundings."

Her frown said it all. She had no tolerance for comments like that.

I explained to her that I had contracted the worst strain of flu in the universe, but her thoughts were elsewhere and my comments washed off her like water off a duck.

"And did you know that a pain in one's small finger means more than all the suffering of mankind –"

I was about to say ... But I thought again ... I would cast my pearls in more appreciative company.

The surgeon was a different kettle of fish. Taking one look at the condition I was in, quipped that he was pretty sure that I was the first to have caught The Millennium Bug – he hoped I would be in better fettle when I arrived for the real thing in February.

I threw off the shirt and despite the heat of the room I shivered like an ivy leaf in front of him. He examined me from top to bottom, asked me the usual health questions, thumped my chest with his fist a few times and informed me that the game was truly on. As I crawled out to the car park I wondered where all my anger had gone. Where is Dylan Thomas when you need him!

People in my situation should be raging to high heaven – genetic gout, peptic ulcer, four operations on my hands and feet, high blood pressure, high cholesterol, eye migraine, liver failure and now a fucking heart by-pass.

And just to put the icing on the cake I have the shagging flu today.

And me being a vegetarian.

I vowed to throw a half dozen sausages on the pan when I got home and fuck the begrudges. It would be the final act of a defeated vegetarian. By the time I reached the car the thought struck me that the wife could be dead in bed when I got home. However if she happened to be alive, I would go out to the back garden and dig up my pipe and tobacco which I had buried there on the day I got the bad news from the cardiologist. In future I was going to live life on my terms and not listen to cock and bull stories about this thing and that thing being good or bad for you. I would get back to the sound and proven philosophy which had no airs or graces

"If you are born to be hanged, you can go to sea in a bucket and you won't be drowned."

Whatever about philosophy this bloody flu had my head all over the place.

Sometimes we are as different from ourselves as we are from other people, and it's probably what differentiates us from the animal kingdom. My old mutt is the same –morning, noon and night, winter or summer, while I can hit the four seasons of humour in any one day. I was glad to find the wife breathing when I got home and thus began the ritual of telling each other how badly we felt all day. We both hit the sack (not for romantic encounters I may add) and tried to hide away from the vicissitudes of life. With the curtains pulled and the grey November light shut out for the afternoon, we fell into the arms of Morpheus leaving flu and doctors and heart operations on the other side of the divide. It was nearly morning when we woke, and with a fair improvement in our respective conditions we were a little bit more equipped to face the world. The wife decided to give work a shot after breakfasting on a glass of orange juice, four cornflakes and two panadol.

Alone again naturally!

The radio was blearing out the Christmas songs and the chirpy voices of those smug little bastards behind the music nearly drove me mad. The thought was slowly brewing that if anything went wrong in the operation this could be my last Christmas. It was the first time I had to seriously face up to my own mortality and it is a difficult process at any age. Sitting on my armchair on the lonesome afternoon brought me back to thoughts of my youth. I remembered my father taking my brother and myself to the Lee fields for a swim. We traveled by bike – me on the front bar and my brother on the back. As we traveled up the Western Road we felt as we were going on Safari; the excitement coursing through our veins. Arriving at The Baths on the Lee Fields we were never able to contain our enthusiasm for getting into the water. As quick as a flash we would strip, scatter our clothes left, right and centre and head for the river just below the weir. My father would gather the clothes, place the bike against the railings of the baths, sit down on the grass, and light up his pipe … and all was well with the world.

"A boy's will is the winds will"

We would splash and dive, and swim and fight until the call came from the shore.

"Baats up."

The prospect of bread and butter drew us from the water like a magnet. We would devour the soft fresh bread and the melted butter – nothing in this world could ever taste better. A quick dry, and back into our corduroy cloths and soon we would be back on board the bike and heading back down the Western Road back to our house in French's Quay.

"And the thoughts of youth are long long thoughts."

It seems so long ago now.

I still have raw anger when I think how unfair is life. My father was never sick a day in his life and yet he was snapped from this world at the age of sixty-one after devoting his entire life to his family. Just when life had turned about, and he could enjoy a little of the comforts of this world he died in his sleep – never even had the time to bid farewell to his family. I looked out the window and the scanty light of the dying afternoon was fading. I looked again. The escaping light from my neighbour's house shaped the shadow of a man on my willow tree … I drew myself closer to the window … I could see more clearly now.

The man in the willow tree wore a cap, and a pipe dangled from his mouth.

He was back to guide me once more!

It was the defining moment for me. Within days we were on the mend from the dreaded flu and the atmosphere had significantly improved in the house. I turned the words of that great American philosopher and writer Ralph Waldo Emersion upside down, inside out, for the solace contained in them

"The light by which we see the world shines from our own souls."

Christmas was coming, the new Millennium was following on its heels, and my big day was in February so I better get myself ready for all the excitement.

I carried the image of the man with the cap and pipe in my head day and night, never mentioning it to another human being – this was my moment of inspiration and my chance to honour my great father by showing some courage. There were still the odd moments, especially in the middle of the night, when haunting thoughts would creep into my mind and these had to be addressed. I summoned up the wise words on courage ... that it was not absence of fear, but carrying on when one is afraid. I was meeting fear head on and the old blighter was losing his stomach for battle.

Life was good – my son was growing up to be a fine young man, my wife was happy and contented and I was looking forward to again been able to walk in the park in the spring. I thought about the daffodils readying themselves to greet me when I finally emerged from my hospital bed, and about the birds singing a special greeting to welcome me and my air shoes back to the park. I would be out on time to see the rabbits frolicking in the morning sunshine, and to see the new–born buds making their first appearance on the trees.

And to see that luscious green carpet of grass, and the scent of spring hanging on the morning air.

Renaissance ... Revival ... Athbeochant an tSaoil !

What a wonderful world!

I want to be around to see it once more.

And I wanted my own renaissance and the fun back in my life. I looked for fun and by God did I find fun. From travelling with mad taxi drivers, to shopping in the aisles of the local supermarkets, and everywhere in between. As I had to put the air shoes into quarantine for the foreseeable future, I re-located myself in the hallowed halls of the local supermarkets. As a House Husband I was perfectly at home in the supermarket setting. I did not have to walk too far and if I felt tired I could lean on the trolley without being counted a real has-been by the other patrons. The atmosphere in the supermarkets was warm and it was refreshing to think that some other person, other than me, was picking up the tab for the heating bill. There was a plentiful supply of Freebie's on offer and the more I became known to the merchandisers in the various shops, the more plentiful was the supply. I had pitched the vegetarian lark to hell and was lashing into the promotional sausages in the aisles to beat the band. Making up for my seven year lapse!

Being a corpulent man already brought its own drawbacks for one contemplating a heart by- pass, but passing through that Operating Theatre door with an extra burden of sausage weight was inexcusable. To this end the wife was like a Tannoy System at a railway station ever chanting about keeping the weight in check. At this stage my bit of writing had dried up like the Goleen mines; for no man could contemplate frolicking about with a typewriter with the vision of a serious operation lurking in the near future. So I had time on my hands.

And the Devil finds work for people with idle hands.

A poor old lady was the first to fall for my madness in the supermarket aisle. It was still November but the Christmas songs were blaring at us and coaxing us to stock up for Christmas lest they run out of goodies. The lady, no bigger than my trolley, was peering at the top shelves, her neck craning.

"Would you mind young man, handing me down a Christmas pudding?" her voice gentle and worn by time. I stood up to my full five feet eight and took down the pudding and pretended to read the label.

"Sorry mam, but you are unable to buy this in November as it is a Christmas product, you can only buy it in December."

I put the pudding back on its resting ground and with a serious look on my face started to move off down the aisle. I looked back from a safe distance to see the woman in uncontrollable laughter. Thus was born one of my great supermarket friendships, for every time I subsequently met her we laughed about the ridiculous event. In between complaining about the wheels on trolleys, questioning the overcharging on the special promotions and being a general pain in the ass for the employees of the supermarkets, I found mischief in other places as well – like the deli counter. I asked a snippy assistant one day for a half pound of cooked ham, she donned her see-through gloves and lifted a number of slices of ham onto the weighing scales. Before she had time to read the scales I cut in,

"You have three quarters of a pound there I said chancing my arm."

With a condescending glance she looked at the reading.

"How did you know that there was three quarters there?" she enquired.

"Because I was a weighing scales in my last existence."

"What kind of a gobshite are you, you must have fuck all else to do," she muttered in her most elegant tone. I stayed clear of the deli counter after that least I get a chopper in the head. Security was now beginning to keep an eye me; for I suspect that information was filtering upstairs that there was a baldy fat man on the prowl and causing mayhem in the supermarket. For me it was a little diversion and an opportunity to take my mind off more important things that were about to happen in the New Year. Shortly afterwards, as I was parking my Ferrari (1992 Carina) in the car park, I got a tap on the window and was told it would be better for me – if I wanted to stay on this side of the great divide – to shag off and do my shopping elsewhere. Thus ended my comic career in the aisles, and I had to return home and leave the supermarkets to the lonely and the sad.

From now onwards I had to pay for my own heating.

CHAPTER NINE

It was a strange Christmas that year. No one in my family wanted to look back, least it might stir up memories, and we were half afraid to look too far into the future. So, we had a quiet Christmas and straight to Cork for the big bash of the New Year – The big bash for the Millennium. At this remove, it is hard to recall again all the hype and fear that this particular day created. We were promised that planes would fall out of the sky at the stroke of twelve, that the ordinary common computer would cease to function, that all hot meals would be suspended due to the fact that cookers would fall dead on the day, and that it was quite likely that it would be the end of civilization as we knew it. So for me, I had the additional worry about coming out alive from my operation, but I had a bigger question to figure out.

Would I have any place to come out to?

The chances were that our world could disappear into thin air following a spate of nuclear explosions. But, as Mr. Franklin once remarked that ninety per cent of the things we worry about never happen. And so it was with the infamous Millennium Bug. Fortunes were made on the backs of silly little people who still prefer to err on the side of caution and spend millions upgrading their equipment. Maybe there was a delayed bug waiting for a smart ass like me, and would strike down the equipment in the operating theatre just as my heart operation began. I was willing to take my chance.

Coming into January any year is a daunting task for you average man or woman in the street. It is well established that it is the most depressing month of the year. This particular January was more depressing than most, after all the hype and lavish partying that went on to celebrate the birth of the new century. Being a House Husband, with very little to do, presented its own problems for me. I thought a lot about the great mystery that is life, and how everything that is alive always comes to an abrupt end in death itself.

'Sceptre and crown must tumble down and in the dust be equal made With the poor crooked scythe and spade.'

My mind being in that mode, shot backwards to my boyhood, and turned up one of the worst days of my life. This was a day that is etched in my memory for many reasons.

During my summer holidays from secondary school, I would normally work with my uncle as a plumber's mate. My uncle's health was very poor mostly from smoking forty fags a day when he was a young man, and now with the advancing years he found himself in that desperate situation where he was unable to walk very far. His employer had the plumbing contract at that stage for the Metropole Hotel in Cork and my uncle was his standard bearer in the hotel, doing all the plumbing work for a very busy hotel. There were a collection of other maintenance men there as well, and each morning I would be detailed to make the tea and everyone would retire to the workshop at the back of the building.   Over the tea break, every problem of the world would be solved and a fair share of lies would get an airing. But the principle business of the day would get top priority – picking out the horses for the Yankees and Trebles and Accumulators. Although I was only fifteen at the time, I soon acquired the knowledge to become a little bit of an expert myself, and with the few bob I got for making the tea and going to the bookies to place the bets, I would have a flutter myself. No one ever asked me my age, all they wanted to see was the colour of the money. There was a guy who was a retired cop who worked locally and I would do the odd docket for him on my rounds. This day he informed me that a horse called 'Early to Rise' had a great chance of winning, but I was to keep my mouth shut about it, and under no circumstance could I tell the maintenance fellows. Of course he won – at ten to one – and I duly collected my winnings. I became more interested now and started delving more closely into the form book; where up to this it was on the hoof betting. The daily routine went on in the hotel and we had our bets every day; winning a few bob here and there.

There was a big renovation taking place in the kitchen which required my uncle and me to work during the night when everything was shut down. We worked from eight in the evening, to eight in the morning, for the six days and I was thrilled when I added up all the double time I would get on top of my wages – riches beyond my wildest dreams. When I collected my big payout the following Thursday my uncle told me to take a half days holiday as a reward for the hard work I put in the previous week. I felt on top of the world and whistled my way towards home. Just as I passed a betting office in Barrack Street I heard the nasally voice calling out the horses. I'll just do a quick Yankee and be on my way. I did my Yankee and just as I was about to leave the attendant betting office clerk behind the counter called out

"Last bets for the commentary race coming up …"

I looked at my bulging pay packet and without thinking threw ten bob on the favourite …. He's still running.

Ten bob was a lot of money to lose, so I went on a rescue mission, but it was me who needed rescuing. I stumbled out the door like a half –dead man after the last race, not a brass penny in the pay packet – skillouched! Lost the lot – every penny.

As the clerk closed the door behind me, he wished me a good

evening. I pulled myself up the few yards to turn into Friars Street and as I moved up the hill, the tears gathered in my eyes and tumbled onto my face. I have never felt so bad or dejected in my life – working all the long hours during those six nights – gone in one afternoon of madness. Straight into the pocket of the bookie.

What kind of a fool was I?

A big bloody one.

I covered my face at the top of Friars Street, least one of my friends or neighbours would see me crying. Fifteen is not a good age for crying in the street, but I just could not control myself. My mother would ask me about the big pay packet, God I had spoken enough about it and what I was going to do with it.

How could I now tell her that I left it all in the bookies. There was no way out but to pretend that I was sick, and that would not be too hard to fake, especially the way I really felt at that stage. When she caught sight of me she knew that there was something wrong other than feeling unwell, but she said nothing as I quickly retired to bed. I did not close my eyes for the entire night as the loss of my money haunted me. There and then I resolved that I would never bet one penny on a horse again during my entire lifetime. The next day at work was just as bad, as I shuffled about, without a brass farthing in my pocket unable to buy a lousy cake. I was unable to go out with my friends at the weekend to the pictures and I stayed in my room under the pretence that I was still feeling under the weather. By Sunday I had to tell my mother the entire story for it was burning up inside me – I told her about my promise never to bet again, and she said it would be a cheap lesson to learn if I stuck to my word. Strange enough I always took a deep interest in the horses, reading about them on the papers and looking at the races on the telly, but I never had an inclination to back a horse again. It must be some yardstick of the hurt I inflicted on myself all those years ago.

But there was one occasion back all those years ago when someone wrote a betting docket on my behalf, and strange to relate, it happened on one of the most fascinating weekends I spent in London. I was working with the Ford Motor Company at the time in Industrial Relations Department, and I went to London on the Friday night in order to take in a bit of entertainment in that lively city. I was working in Dagenham Plant on the Monday morning – just an old doss for the day – and returning on the Tuesday. Flying out of Cork in 1973 was easier than taking the number three bus, as there was so little traffic in the airport. The occasional plane coming-in and going-out, a few strollers grabbing food on the hoof, and customs guys that always waved you on irrespective of whether you were coming or going. I arrived in Heathrow Airport and waited by the carousel to collect my luggage … and waited … and waited.

Not a sausage!

By this stage the area had emptied and slowly it was dawning on me that my luggage was not going to turn up.   I was left in my casual street clothes and nothing else. What would I do for Monday? I could not arrive at the Dagenham plant wearing a canary- coloured shirt. After making my lost property report I headed for my hotel in London.

Second disaster of the day!

The fecking lights were all turned off in the capital – there was some kind of strike so we were all cast into absolute darkness. Now this situation called for some ingenuity to resolve. I needed to do some shopping and I needed to get a suit for work on Monday morning. It is hard for me – being the worst clothes shopper in the world – to buy a suit at the best of times, but trying to buy a suit by candlelight was a severe challenge. The Cockney shop assistant walked round me with the candle, saying how wonderful this particular suit looked on me. Though I was not sure what colour it was, never mind the cut, I decide to go for it – Hobson's Choice.

I gave him my Barclay card, and with the determination of an Everest Climber, he managed to complete the paperwork and charge up the dough. He threw some wrapping on the suit and as I was about to find my way out, he quipped that you would think the suit was made by a tailor. I grabbed another few odds and ends and headed for the hotel in a taxi. The lights in the hotel were working – they had their own generator – and having booked in, returned to the bar to ponder the whereabouts of my luggage. When I rang the airport I was informed that the luggage had taken a trip to Hong Kong and would return in a day or two. I sat in the bar and peered into my pint. Then I peered into another pint. This could be one of those boring nights – and in London of all places. Suddenly the main door of the hotel was flung open and I heard mad voices in the foyer.

Christ they sound like Irish voices.

Limerick voices to be more precise, and by God were they on the tear. Four or five of them rushed into the bar and shouted for pints. The advanced party was quickly joined by the main body, which seemed to be struck down with the same thirst.

There was an energy and verve about them that, if it could be harnessed, would relight London.

"Throw a pint at that man down there," said one of the lads who was ordering the drink, not knowing me from Adam.

"Up the Rebels," I shouted in his direction.

"For fuck sake, we can't get away from you bastards, pull up your stool here and join us, you're like a forgotten soul down there."

I was never a man who required a second invitation.

Soon the sing–song was beginning to get legs much to the astonishment of the other patrons in the bar, but it did not take long for them to be drawn into the merriment, such was the quality of their singing and their infectious good humour. I have been to many sing-songs in my day, but I can say with certainty that I have never heard a better bunch of singers anywhere on the planet. They were members of the Shannon Rugby Club and they had come to London for the international match with England the following day.

"Look we have a few spare tickets for the match, would you fancy coming with us tomorrow, we'll be going by coach."

Would I what!

The merriment went on late into the night and I hit the sack at about three o'clock, having consumed a fair cargo of Guinness. The thought of lost luggage was the last thing on my mind. Outside my hotel room the lights of the city were making a re-appearance as my lights were disappearing for the night. Saturday morning came with undue haste, and I woke with the father and a mother of a hangover. My tongue was as dry as the Gobi desert and continued to stick to my pallet as if drawn by a magnet. I searched for water but there was not a drop of any kind of liquid in the room. On with the trousers and shirt, dive under the bed to retrieve the shoes and soon I was heading in the direction of the bar once more. The cockney barman of the previous evening was still in situ; he smiled when he saw me. Great night last night – that was some sing–song. "Forget last night for Christ sake, get me a beer shandy, my tongue is about to fall out of my head with the thirst." The large brass clock over the bar read eleven o'clock. A few of the night revelers came into the bar.

"Too late for the breakfast inside," they shouted at the barman.

"You were too late an hour ago mate, hop up on those stools and I'll pour a couple of pints and I'll go and see if they have anything left in the kitchen."

Soon we were all slugging down porter again, and when it linked up with the previous nights intake we were merry in no time. And the cockney barman true to his word, had the sausages and bacon in front of us in no time. This guy was a real star. We were nicely set up now for the coach ride to Twickenham. By now the whole place was buzzing with the melodic sound of Limerick accents. Just as the coach arrived the barman informed me that he was going across the road to do a bet and did I want him to place a bet for me. The drink had kicked in by now, and me forgetting my promise, told him to do a Yankee and to include any Irish horses running in England that day on the docket.

"I'll settle up with you later, once we beat the arse off England."

The coach started up, the singing started and we were on our way. We were in buoyant mood at the match cheering on the men in green. During play the pitch was invaded by people protesting about the hunger strike in Northern Ireland. When the game resumed it was a cracker. Kevin Flynn went over for a try in the last few minutes, and against all the odds, Ireland won the game. We were delirious in the crowd celebrating the famous victory. Back in the coach and the real singing began, and continued right up to us arriving at our hotel. We had our dinner and it was back to the bar for one rip-roaring evening. The cockney barman called me to the end of the counter.

"That was some luck you had."

"Jez, we were haunted in the end, good old Kevin Flynn," I replied.

"Not the bloody match mate, you won two hundred quid on the horses!"

He reached into his back pocket and handed me a wad of money.

"It's all there intact, I just deducted the price of the docket … you had four winners; the three Irish horses won at good prices, you lucky sod."

He absolutely refused to take one brass farthing from me. Even when I pushed the money into his top pocket, he quickly returned it to me. After the loss of my luggage this was turning out to be a good weekend. The Shannon guys refused to take a penny for the coach or the match ticket even after I informed them of my good luck on the gee gees. The celebrations went on into the night and on Sunday morning their coach set out for the airport with a weary but happy bunch.

It was, for me, the most profitable weekend of my life. Fords paid for all my weekend expenses, the horses came up with the unexpected bonus, and Aer Lingus refunded me for the loss of my luggage.

And we beat England!

CHAPTER TEN

Counting down the days, to my operation date of February the Ninth, was a slow and sometimes painful exercise. The daffodils should be peeping up about then – Christ I hope I won't be peeping up as well. The cold January delayed the birth of the daffodils, and they were still asleep when I at last checked in at the hospital on the night before the operation. When all the necessary hospital forms were signed and completed, and when I finally agreed that in the case of me dying, it would be no one else's fault but my own for not waking up, I signed. If they had thrown The Treaty of Versailles and The Treaty of Limerick in front of me that day I would have put my name to those as well.

After all the preliminaries were over in the Admissions Office, I was taken to the Cardiac Ward to await my destiny with the knife in the morning. The ward was small and contained four beds, but there was only one other patient other than myself. My room-mate looked a miserable specimen of humanity – his dressing gown hung on him like a drooping coat on a cloths line. And, in direct contrast to yours truly, he looked as if he weighed about seven stone. He was faced towards the wall as if he was praying but on hearing my noisy arrival, turned round to greet me by tipping his cap in my direction. At least his eyesight seems to be intact, I thought, but by all accounts it was the only thing that was functioning with him. I was amazed by the strength of his voice.

"I'm totally bollixed since this crowd did a job on me over a month ago now – pain everywhere in my shagging body."

I donned a sympathetic look as if I was interested in his health – I had more pressing things on my own mind.

"Look, I'll show you the scar on my chest," he began to open his shirt.

That did it for me.

"If you open another button on that fucking shirt I'll have you thrown out of here by security."

"Jez, you're a touchy one," he went on.

This was some resting ward; with that lunatic in residence, it was more like a stress factory. But things got better when the hospital Sister visited me, and set out my programme of events up to the big incision moment. I settled down in the bed with the paper, while my room-mate turned his face to the wall once more.

More prayers or gripes at the Wailing Wall!

A tap on the door and a tall figure in black was heading in my direction – the Chaplain very kindly came to visit me. And if I was nervous before, I was practically shitting myself now, with the sight of the Padre.

"James, I came along to see if you wanted to receive the Sacraments. I believe you are getting the big job done tomorrow morning."

"Father," said I, "wouldn't I be the real hypocrite if I wanted to receive the Sacraments at this time, and me not having been to Mass or Confession for twenty-five years? If there was a God up there, what would he make of me?"

The Padre smiled.

"You're a typical Corkman, never lost the accent and obstinate to the very end."

The Chaplain and myself were close together as human beings, though I suspect he was further up the religious ladder than myself. But this was no time to open up a discussion on the existence of God, either way I was about to have my day in the Theatre whether God was alive or dead. The Chaplain was a very affable man. He pulled up his chair and we had a good chat about everything under the sun except religion. When the tea lady stuck her head round the door a half an hour later, the Padre rose to his feet, wished me well, threw a blessing in the direction of the other patient and with a wonderful smile left the room. I knew in my bones that this man had found something special for himself on this planet. Faith is a greater virtue than reason, I thought to myself, as I munched on my toast. I made a phone call to my poor wife at home, who by now was stricken with fear, just to reassure her that all was well on the western front. All logic would suggest that I should be peppering with apprehension, if not fear, but I was as calm and cool as the proverbial cucumber. By now the room-mate deserted the Wailing Wall and had settled himself in bed still muttering about the bloody bastards. I brought half the county library books into the hospital with me but somehow I just could not concentrate, so in the quietude of the ward I just lay back on my pillow and tried to pick out faces on the yellow ceiling. Suddenly I felt this hand on my shoulder. I woke abruptly, and a young man with a shaven head and broad smile was looking into my eyes.

"Mr. Archer, my name is John, I'm here to prepare you for your operation tomorrow."

It took me a few seconds to get my bearings, having dozed off.

"Glad to meet you, sorry I nodded off there."

"Good to see you are relaxed; this will take about an hour all together."

He pulled the screens, dispatched me to the shower and got his instruments of war ready for my re-appearance. He pointed out that I had to be shaved from head to toe and everywhere else in between. The head was baldy enough so that would not present too much of a problem, but I was fearful about shaving round the old Gap of Dunloe. Isn't it amazing how hair will grow profusely in every part of the body except on the head where it's supposed to grow. He started to shave my chest, and he was removing hair by the bucket load; it was like clearing the Amazon jungle. It is not the best feeling in the world to have your entire body shaved by a man – I'm not sure what it would be like if it was a woman who held the razor – but that's another area of human experience altogether. When I feel uncomfortable, my motto has always been to get back to the old yoga. So I lay back on the bed, closed my eyes, and brought up a picture of Banna Strand on a warm sunny day. I was the only soul on the beach and as I went deeper into my meditation, all I could hear was the sound of the waves as they lapped the shore and the occasional cry of a seagull in the distance. Despite my concentration on this tranquil scene, I was now conscious that John had now moved downstairs to the sensitive parts with the razor. Suddenly my room-mate let out an almighty bark which caused me to jump in the bed and the razor just missed cutting off my retributary cudgel. John my shaver just stood there with the razor held above my body,

"That was a close one," he muttered.

"Jez, I came in for a heart by-pass, I did not expect to be gelded as well."

We both laughed and that took the heat out of the situation. Meanwhile, the cause of the anguish – old bag of bones himself – was fast asleep in his bed, and snoring now, if you don't mind.

The shaving exercise went full steam ahead and I returned to Banna Strand until John eventually finished.

"There you go," said John, "all ready for the Christmas market."

I ran my hand down my entire body.

"Jez, your right, I do feel like a plucked turkey."

When John had gathered up the hair, and put his instruments of war – razor, brush and shaving cream back in their respective homes in his carry bag – he thanked me for my patience, wished me well for the following day and said he would return with a toupee.

"I'm not going down that road again," I said

"Too much heartache."

He disappeared out the door and left me with my thoughts and a shiny hairless body.

But I was not left alone for long.

The nurses came at me. While most men of my age would welcome the intrusion of a gentle female presence; for me it was not pleasurable. I had too many thoughts in my head and too little hair on my body. But these girls were old hands dealing with old codgers like me.

"You'll have a new crop for the summer," is how one of the nurses put it, when I explained how strange it felt to be as bare as a new born baby.

"Throw up your arm there, we have a bucket of blood to take from you yet."

The warm smile, and the gentle caress of the hand, and all was right with the world. When she had taken a sufficient quantity of the red stuff from my tired old body she vamoosed, only to have hard on her heels another Florence Nightingale, this time to check my blood pressure.

Believe me this was some resting ward!

Another phone call to my poor embattled wife to again re-assure her that I was over the preliminaries. All was on track, and it was full steam ahead for the morning. I told her about my mishap with the razor and how I nearly lost my Johnny Do-Da, and how my room-mate – old bag of bones – was the greatest sleeper either side of the Atlantic. He slept through all the comings and the goings of the nurses in the ward. Whatever his list of medical complaints he had after his operation, sleep deprivation would not find its way onto his medical chart. as soon as I put down the phone I had another visitor at my bedside – this time a doctor.

"A final few checks," he said.

Ye – more like two pages of questions!

And another Treaty to sign, after all that lot. I refused another supper of tea and toast, accepted the two sleeping tablets from the nurse; head on the pillow and goodbye cruel world.

As if I was pre-programmed I woke at six on the dot, realized after a few seconds where I was, and furthermore what I was here for – the day when my heart would be repaired. I thought of my wife and son and wondered if they slept as well as me. "Didn't close my eyes all night," she told me, when I phoned her; my son slept like all boys' his age.

The hospital team was on my case pretty soon – in no time I was heading for the shower. As I passed the long mirror I looked at myself – Christ it was enough to give anyone a heart attack. A rotund hairless creature peered back at me; it could have been someone from a Hitchcock movie. I washed my slippery frame and sought the safety of the bath towel when I heard the nurse arriving.

"All right in there, Jim?"

"It's taking me time to get used to my new body," I replied.

"Let's be having you out here, time is moving on."

Everything in the hospital was now moving into full gear except Bag of Bones – he was still firmly in the arms of Morpheus. The cleaners were shunting beds hither and thither, as they cleaned and polished everything in sight. Soon the attention switched to me – the main act for that day. Two Florence Nightingales were detailed to get me into shape for the short journey to the theatre. Another quick call to the wife,

"I'm still great, no nerves no nothings."

Another round of blood pressure checks, the final fitting of the gown I was about to wear at the gig, a jab in the arse and I was on my way. As I was wheeled down the corridor, I hoped the surgeon wasn't on the piss the night before – we need steady hands and steady nerves at this stage. The surgical team were all dressed up and ready to go. I was greeted with a quiet word and a nod, and my ample carcass was maneuvered onto the sacrificial altar. A prod in my arm and my lights shut down, and vanished in a swirling manner, just like water disappearing down a plughole.

Orate pro nobis!

All our family dreams for the future depended on the skill of these wonderful people.

Orate pro nobis!

Someone did, for I woke up in intensive care.

Though my head was hazy and full of sleep I knew that I had woken up on the right side of the divide – there was no sign of the Quare Fellow with the horns – so I guessed I was safe for now. My family was just allowed a peep at me, as I drifted from one sleep to another – time like myself had fallen asleep on that February afternoon. When I eventually did wake up for any period, it was late evening, and as I looked round me for the first time, I noticed that I had more attachments than a Dyson Vacuum Cleaner. Two nurses were taking my readings with such vigour and purpose they could have been controlling the national grid.

"Am I alive or what?"

"You're very much alive, the operation was a fantastic success," replied the nurse

"Your surgeon will have a word with you later on; he has already spoken to your wife and relayed the good news."

But my waking was short lived – when I woke again it was the first anniversary of my operation – exactly one day!

And my wife and her sister were at my bedside, smiling like Cheshire cats. The prognosis was excellent after a very successful operation and all my readings were normal already – there was even talk of moving me out of intensive care that evening. As soon as they left the tea and toast appeared and I ate my first bite of food – I was on the mend and moving fast.

Getting out of the intensive care boosted my confidence, but just as I was growing cocky I was hit with a severe dose of gout in my hands and legs. Unfortunately the doctors were unable to give me any medication for the gout, as they feared it was too dangerous so close to the operation.

So I had to suffer along.

The intensity of the pain would drive the tears out my eyes, and to me it was a metaphor for my life – just as I had jumped one hurdle along comes another. It was always that way. However within a few days the doctors were in a position to prescribe the medicine for the gout, and the pain melted away like the snows of winter. After eight days I was ready for the road.

With my kind of luck I might even reach sixty.

Arriving home for the first time felt strange – somehow I felt as if I had been away for a very long time. After resting for a few days, I threw on the air shoes and, with my wife by my side, started out on my walk – this time with a re-conditioned heart.

My recovery was well and truly underway.

CHAPTER ELEVEN

In sickness and in health!

If ever a maxim was tested it surely was the situation with my wife. She had seen me slide from an extraordinary fit thirty-four year old who played squash five times a week and ran like a maniac through Phoenix Park on the other two days, to someone who was unable to get out of bed due to the severity of the pain. On top of this I had to surrender my job, give up my ambition to do well and of course give up my prospects of earning money. I suppose I am lucky in a sense that seeing a Ferrari in the driveway to impress the neighbours was never an ambition of mine.

As Mr. Shakespeare remarked,

'Wisdom cries out in the street and no man regards it.'

My deterioration in health was rapid and uncompromising, and the scope and variety of illness's that visited me were frightening. Now I was starting back once more on the road to recovery with a scar dissecting my chest and nasty hole in my leg running from my upper thigh to my ankle – well I suppose it beats the arse out of the alternative.

So it was air shoes for my wife and air shoes for me!

We were assured by all the medics that exercise was the best path to a speedy recovery, and having been given a second shot at this life, I was determined to take it. The wife was at my side more often than my guardian angel walking in hail, rain and snow and I was inching forward on the recovery meter. When we first met all those years ago, we could not have had any idea how things might work out. I was in my early twenties and doing nicely in the Ford Motor Company – a nice car, plenty of spondulux and very little sense. After the wedding of one of my mates from the athletic club, we went for "afters" to Constitution Rugby Club. Needless to say we were in tip top form after the wedding. During the night I spotted my prey, asked her to dance, she smelt my alcoholic breath while dancing, made her excuses and skedaddled. At the end of the night, as a few of the wedding party were rawmeshing outside the door of the club, this car pulled up and waited outside the door to pick up someone. Me, being in high spirits hopped into the car and there she was again! I could not believe my luck. Finally to get me out of the car we made a pact, and I deserted the car on the proviso that we would meet the following Friday night. Her friend Rita who was driving the car, and herself, would meet my friend Kieran and myself. They would have agreed to meet Attila the Hun and his father in order to get the car free. But promises are promises and she possessed the same honourable word as me and low and behold, they did turn up on Friday night. Everything went great and we all got on fantastically well, and in the coming weeks Veronica and myself; and Rita and Kieran; struck up relationships. Later on that year I struck out for Paris and in the midst of the intervening years we lost complete touch with each other touch. But I always remembered her, and thought a lot about her, when I was in Paris. Six years later when I was back in Cork I got a phone call.

"Would I attend the "afters" at Blackrock Castle?"– Believe it or not, Rita and Kieran were getting married. I went for a pint to my local on the Friday night, and half way through the evening I remembered the phone call. I had completely forgotten about the wedding. Christ, I was dressed for nothing but a game of darts; however these minor matters never stopped me doing anything before in my life. I made a decision – I would go out on the street and if I could pick up a taxi within five minutes I would join the merry band of revelers at the wedding.

A taxi duly arrived and picked me up, and soon I was on my way to Blackrock Castle wearing a jumper. I made my grand entrance, no one made a comment about my attire, I drank a few pints, sang a few songs, met up with Veronica again and married her a few months later.

Snappy or what?

Now here she was again twenty years later, having ridden out all the vicissitudes that life had thrown in our direction, back at the coalface once more, and creeping out of the dark hole and looking for the bright sunshine of hope. The appearance of the daffodils helped lift our spirits on those walks; we pondered on their survival over the long winter, and being true to their calling appeared each year in their new beautiful attire.

And I was growing stronger by the day.

At this rate of progress it would be no time before I would be back to abnormality again. The March Lion was slowly giving way to the gentler Lamb, and the fair daffodils were once again hearing the call to return to nature once more.

I was well enough to get behind the wheel of the car once more, thereby giving me back a mighty load of freedom. I was truly amazed when I ventured on the scales, that for all that tea and toast period, I had not lost one single pound in weight.

I was still the rotund baldy man with the superior complex, now brandishing two war wounds. When one feels boredom it is a sure sign that recovery is almost complete, so one day, when I received a lucky phone call asking me to do some Creative Writing Classes,

I jumped at the opportunity. It was the perfect anti-dote to my rehabilitation classes. From my experience over the years, I found that all writing classes are basically the same when they start out. The would–be writers all believe that they have a special talent, and that at last they are moving into an arena that will bring them fame and fortune beyond their wildest dreams. So, my strategy was to leave them to their own devices for a few weeks until they sort themselves out. Of course, I would encourage them to continue to write, but basically I am on my guard for the smartass to appear. My new group was a mixture of the old and the young, both male and female – a perfect combination to get sparks going in the class.

And it did not take long.

This small, fat woman with white hair and a clipped English accent was the first to emerge. She was somehow under the impression that the classes were convened so that she had a readymade audience for her scribblings, which she had written over the years. She always positioned herself at the other end of the table to me, and as soon as the class started she was like a greyhound out of the trap. She began to read her piece to the assembled class in tones that would not be out of place on BBC Radio Four. She read and she read and if I left her she'd be reading still.

"Now, now, hold your horses there 'til we get a comment from the other people in the class."

She reluctantly stopped.

"Well Jacinta, what do you think of what Margaret has written?"

"To be perfectly honest," she answered in her best Liberties accent,

"I think its pure crap."

That did it – the third world war was about to break out.

Everyone burst into laughter. Margaret's eyes just doubled in size, the veins stood out on her fleshy neck as a crimson glow enveloped her face.

Tread softly for you tread on my dreams!

She was off!

"How dare an unmarried mother from the slums of Dublin use that language about my work let me, here and now, tell you hussy that I was Head Mistress in an exclusive English school for over thirty years …"

"But you never learned to write English," Jacinta cut in.

That did it.

"Class is over for this week," I shouted in desperation. It had barely started.

"Hopefully when we return next week we'll be all cooler around the collars."

I turned on my heels and left the uproar and chaotic scenes behind. This was no place for a soul recovering from open heart surgery. As I drove towards the hospital to do my yoga exercises as part of the rehabilitation programme, I pondered on the job as creative writing tutor to this lot. I had taken up the position to cure my boredom, but I probably bit off more than I could chew. Perhaps it would be safer to be decked out in a helmet for the next installment in the class. As usual, our rehab programme always began with a talk by one of the team of health specialist – today it was the turn of the cardiologist. As he moved to the podium, the twenty or so participants sat in a circle round him – and we hung on every word.

"Today I am about to ask you all a question."

We waited in anticipation.

"Why have you lot got coronary heart disease?"

A few brave souls ventured forth with a few ideas.

"Overweight, bad diet, no exercise."

The old hardy annuals were trotted out.

"Let me tell you, here and now, the reason you are all before me is that you have chosen the wrong parents."

A few chuckles from the audience.

"Yes, my dear friends I will tell you this, you have no reason to feel that you alone are totally responsible for your disease."

This was my kind of man – no bullshit – just tell the truth.

He went on to talk about the other factors, but any little semblance of guilt I felt that in some way I might have been the architect of my own misfortune lifted off my shoulders and propelled me forward to attack life with a greater vigour.

I once again engaged the old mantra,

With my dying breath may I say I'll start again.

Of course life is about starting all over again. Days and weeks roll around, months tumble into years, and years just repeat – I must get this point home to the writing class that life is about starting again – especially those who never got a start.

It was with great trepidation that I looked forward to the next gathering of the writers class. Jacinta was unable to get a baby sitter so the bold Margaret, ever-ready for battle, visualized having a clear run at this session. One exercise I gave the class to do was to retire to a quiet spot, armed with a bunch of blank sheets of paper and to write, starting with their earliest memory, and moving forward in time without paying any attention to grammar or spellings, but to just get ideas flowing along on the pages. Margaret thought this was a stupid idea, for how could one write English without paying attention to grammar and spellings. She was becoming a right pain in the neck, for all she wanted to do was to showcase what she had written herself. But she tangled with the wrong man. I asked her to collect her manuscripts and her attitude and to kindly, "fuck off out of the class." She threatened everyone on me, from the Garda Commissioner to the Minister for Justice and everyone else in between, but in the end she upped sails and departed to the cheers of her classmates. Now we get down to serious work. Though most of the people in the class had left school without completing their education, they showed an incredible appetite and application to get stuck in and learn. I was continuously driving home the point to them, the importance of finding their own voices, and to express how they saw the world through their own eyes.

Meanwhile I was seeing the world through rehab eyes myself, as I was slowly put through my paces about the new me – the post operation me – and how to proceed with my life and not to be a cardiac cripple. I certainly had no intention of becoming one of those. My walking was now up to three miles a day and increasing both in mileage and intensity. I was returning to the same old boring cocky bastard the wife said. On hearing this, I knew my recovery was almost complete. By now the writing class was showing promise and one or two of them had published stories in the local magazines, and had their eyes set on higher things. Just a few weeks into the classes and something remarkable was happening with the bunch – the confidence levels, particularly among the younger set in the class, were rising by the week. This metamorphosis was happening before my very eyes and it was wonderful to behold – they had some hope for the first times in their lives. Seeing this gave me a new impetus to work even harder to help them, and this was rewarding and fulfilling for me as well. There was this woman in the class, who put her heart and soul into everything she did; she wrote an essay depicting the horrible life she had encountered. She had suffered physical and mental abuse at the hands of her husband for many years. She was determined to change her life and to this end she had taken up yoga, and had attended many courses on self-help and, eventually being happier in herself, had become a much kinder person. But, eventually, she had to get rid of the husband by securing a barring order against him, and the police had to evict him onto the street. When he returned one night in the pouring rain, he knocked at the front door hoping to get some refuge for the night; she poked her head out the upstairs window and told him to fuck off with love.

This is exactly the way I felt at my yoga classmate down at the rehab clinic. The relaxation guru was taking us through our paces as part of our programme, and armed with our floor mats and our enthusiasm, we made our way to a quieter part of the hospital – this motley collection of human crocks – all in search of peace and harmony. After many minutes of coughing and shuffling about on the floor the team was ready for inaction.

'Close your eyes gently … lie back and feel your body sinking … feeling more comfortable and warm now …'

The melodic tones of Mozart now rising in the background, as the guru's voice becomes even slower, quieter and more deliberate.

'Concentrate on the head now … gently remove those creases from your forehead …' he went on.

The feeling was wonderful … Lovely feelings of peace and tranquility were washing over my body …

Suddenly, he started. Gently at first, but within seconds rising to an almighty crescendo – the bastard was snoring to high heaven.

My fecking peace was gone out the window and I was back to my old self – I wanted to kill the fucker on the spot. The Guru eventually woke him up, and we all started back on the relaxation trail once more. But no sooner had we started when the trumpet started up again. I thought beheading was now a far better option. The exercise was ruined, the time was wasted and the programme shagged up, but old whiskey nose just rose from the mat, and casual as you like, bid us all a good day and disappeared out the door.

Strange to relate but I was finding more peace and tranquility at the writing classes than at the yoga classes. There was a great feeling of unity and camaraderie amongst the group and opinions on peoples work was given without the special branch having been brought in for protection. This was always an ongoing problem with other groups I had been associated with in the past; very few people could take a negative critique without getting snotty-nosed. This lot ware different, and an absolute joy to be associated with – they knew it was not where you start but where you finish is the important thing. I had a habit of quoting various things off the cuff and this day I mentioned that the motto of the Bolshoi Ballet was that:

'Movement was life'

To my absolute astonishment this young girl Sarah burst into tears. I asked her if she was OK and if she wanted to leave the room, fearing that something might be amiss at home. She waved her head and the class continued. After the class was over and after the others had departed the room, she approached me and apologised for causing a disturbance in the class. I told her not to be silly.

She told me that she was now the mother of a small boy and when she became pregnant her mother had thrown her out of her home. The mention of the Bolshoi Ballet brought all the memories back because she had trained to be a ballet dancer for many years.

Her mother always had the hope that she might one day become a professional dancer, and when she had become pregnant her mother was so disappointed with her that she shunted her out of her home and out of her life. She now had a shabby bed sit and lived all alone with her son.

When we were well into the course I was informed that regretfully, due to lack of funding, the creative writing classes would have to be closed down. The disappointment was palpable in the classroom. They had invested so much of their time and energy and, just as it was about to take off for them, the bloody thing had to be stopped – just for the sake of a few quid. But many vowed that once the writing bug had got a grip on them they were not about to let it drop now. I told them I was always at the other end of a phone line to help. Thus ended the creative writing class of 2000, the magic year of the new century – you may call it a new year, you may call it a new century, but the old school who control the purse-strings never change.

I wrote to over twenty people including the leading politicians explaining the situation, but as they used to say in Cork long ago, I might as well have pissed against the wind.

The rehab continued for some time after the writing classes got the chop, and at this stage we were sufficiently well enough to attack the gym. From my experience with gyms and the lunatics that frequent them, I was hoping against all hope that we might be spared the antics especially in the controlled setting of the hospital.

But, I was wrong.

Seeing that our bunch were recovering from treble heart by-passes, double by–passes, enlarged hearts, heart attacks, malfunctioning valves and so on, one would have thought that they would not set the gym alight with their athletism. Two trained nurses stood by and attached the 'athletes' to the heart monitoring apparatus. Blood pressures were taken for each 'athlete' and the fun began. There were five pieces of apparatus and each person had to spend two minutes working out on each piece which meant we all had to start out at the same time – but there was one missing.

"Rosetta, who has seen Rosetta?" said the nurse.

"Here I am, on my way."

Nonchalantly, she made her entrance.

I was Moulin Rouge trained in my younger days, and saw many things on my travels, but no one would hold a candle to our Rosetta. Even though she was approaching forty, she had the face and body of a well-developed twenty year old. She wore the tightest silk pants that clung like a lizard to her long tanned legs, while her skimpy top hardly contained her massive tits.

"Jesus," said old Charlie, "she'd give anyone a heart attack, and I thought I was coming to a safe environment."

"She had a valve replaced in her heart only a month ago," said the nurse to a few of us, gawking from a distance.

"The bitch better hurry, she's holding up everything," muttered the nurse.

She was now growing catty – the attention was switching elsewhere. As soon as the divine Rosetta was hooked up to the monitor, the show could get on the road. Now, there existed in the group, a large lump of man from the West of Ireland who was always in a hurry, "this fucking exercise thing is costing me money," he kept repeating.

God only knows why he turned up at all, but there he was all six foot six of him decked out in a workman's overalls and a three-day growth on his face. He was a fearsome man to look at, never mind to tangle with, so he won the race among the Pilgrims to be the follow up to Rosetta on the machine sequence. In this way – The Large Lump had a first class view of Rosetta as she suggestively put herself about on the machines. Old Charlie who had the happy knack of knowing everything about everyone remarked that this was dangerous for a lump of a man who already had three heart attacks and he still not forty.

And he was right!

For no sooner had Rosetta hit the cross-over machine and The Lump started on the rowing machine when the shaggin' monitor alarm went off. Rosetta got such a start that she jumped clear of the machine, and in doing so split her pants straight up the middle. But the nurses went rushing towards The Lump for it was his monitor that was roaring to high heaven. His blood pressure had gone through the roof. In five minutes he was residing in intensive care ward of the hospital with a team of doctors working like demented ducks round him. Rosetta was covering her modesty with Charlie's overcoat and wondering if someone could give her a lift home. But we all saw what happened to The Lump and one by one sneaked out the back door of the hospital with our hearts intact for the moment.

When I returned home I received a very surprising phone call. It was from Sarah – the young girl from the writing class – and she was letting me know that there were great developments in her circumstances. When the classes had finished and she was alone in her bedsit, she somehow drew up the courage to contact her mother. She sent one of her ballet shoes with a photo of her young baby placed inside the shoe, and a little note of greeting to her mother. The mother melted and things started to happen. She was back in her comfortable home; she was hatching plans to return to education, she might even start back dancing again. She said, that when she was alone at night she thought a lot about the old motto 'that movement was life' and realised that if she was to have any life, never mind any prospects, she better do some moving herself. Thus, she conceived the idea of sending the shoe.

Now, unlike Rosetta, that news did my heart good!

With the creative writing class closed down, and the rehabilitation programme completed, I had no option but to return to my full time vocation which the insurance company so graciously bestowed on me all those years ago – I was a full time House Husband once more. On my fortieth birthday I realised that I had achieved very little in my life, now into my fifties and with the big six-o looming in the distance I was once again stuck in a Limbo. The excitement coming up to the operation and the subsequent operation itself concentrated the mind – The Hangman's Concentration – like nothing before in my life. Now returning to a situation where I could walk once more was a fantastic feeling, and I was grateful to all who got me there. Now back on the homestead, I was doing the old chores once more, here where mundane things take on an importance of their own. Cooking the rustic stew, putting the bin out on Thursday morning, answering the door for every kind of conman and salesman, beating the same persistent bastards off the phone became the top priorities in my life.

I needed to escape.

Increasingly I found myself ambling through the many parks in my area. The fair daffodils had long departed, and all that remained to remind us of their beauty were the green stems – but they too would soon depart under the blades of the tractor. The more time I spent alone with the trees and the flowers and of course the wild animals, the more I knew in my heart that I was seeking something else – perhaps a more spiritual dimension to my life. The conventional religions left me cold, and I found more solace in the fields than anywhere else – I was reconnecting with nature. Perhaps I was becoming a Pantheist as distinct from a Pantyist – of whom there are many avid followers about. Taking to the parks early in the morning became a real delight. That first fresh feeling of the day, the smell of newly cut grass, the rabbits scattering in all directions, and the colours; 'yellow, and black and pale and hectic red.'

And the music of the birds!

Could this be heaven? It might be part of it.

Include the mighty trees – majestically stretching into the blue sky. While I was strolling one morning I saw to my horror that one the big oak trees had fallen during the storm of the previous night. There it lay at my feet having given up the ghost after all those years.

What it had seen in its lifetime.

For the rest of my walk I could not get the image of that tree out of my mind – it felt as if a friend had died. With a heavy heart, I returned home and some weeks later wrote this poem:

OBITUARY

On Monday last in Corkagh Park
An elderly tree collapsed and died
(Natural causes)
Removal will take place
In coming week
By nearby residents
To be cremated in suburban fireplaces
Sadly missed by birds rats flies creepy crawlies
A host of other friends
Word of thanks to
Sun rain and earth for
Sustaining
A treasured life

CHAPTER TWELVE

Quo vadis?

I have always been fascinated by those two words.

Where goest thou? The two most challenging words one is likely to hear in a lifetime. However only slightly behind, in order of importance, is the other question,

Where comest thou from?

I came from a 'Mystery' … a Mystery House to be more precise.

On the day that I was born, 17 January 1947, if I could have looked out my window, I would have seen the River Lee gurgling along below me. You see I was born, literally, on the Banks of the Lee during the coldest winter in living memory. When the windows of my birth room were flung open on that afternoon to release the accompanying fumes that I brought into the world with me, I must have imbibed the dark tangy aroma of Beamish Stout rising up from the brewery not thirty feet across the river – for to this day; I still love to caress its creamy head.

I must have been The Devil himself – for within a few weeks of my birth, my poor mother had to go to be churched in 'the South Chapel'. She had to be cleaned, washed out, and forgiven by Christ himself, for bringing such a monstrous little devil into the world. And she had to leave a donation behind her to ensure that all other offending women in the future would have a church to go to, where they could receive the same steam cleaning from God for committing such a heinous act of bringing a child into the world.

I was born in a house that glorified in the title of 'Crosses Green House' It had fifteen large rooms, walled gardens with imposing gates, and to the side, as I mentioned we had our own river, while to the front we had our courtyard. We could have been aristocracy.

There was just one problem.

We had to share this house with eight other families, all with the same high fertility rates as ourselves. The people in the surrounding streets always referred to our house as 'The Mystery House.' The myth grew up in the area, that everyone who ever walked from French's Quay down through Crosses Green always turned into 'The Mystery House' but stranger still was the fact that no one was ever seen coming out of the house. If my family was poor we certainly did not realise it. We were pretty much the same as everyone else around us. By this stage our family had settled at a nice rounded figure of eight, which meant that space was now the principal preoccupation of my parents. Although we had three very large rooms, one would need a good grasp of geometry to carve up this space to accommodate four girls, two boys and both my parents. But as necessity is the mother of invention this was somehow achieved, and we had to get on with the serious business of growing up.

And what a house to grow up in!

Like something straight out of a Hitchcock film. Three flights of unlit creaking stairs, with big brown doors at every turn and danger lurking round every corner.

I still remember the terror whenever I had to negotiate those dark stairs alone, nerves jangling and my imagination out of control; until I would reach the safety of our front door at the very top of the house. The dim yellowy gaslight of our sitting room was as welcome as the blazing lights of New York. But life for my parents was far from glamorous. The hungry fifties were certainly to be seen all round. My mother had to cook for eight people on an open fire, no need to tighten the belt in that house – it was always a race to the table. No wonder I turned out to be one of the best sprinters in the country later on; I had plenty of early training. It is impossible to visualise how difficult life was in the fifties. Hitler had got his come-uppence in the war, but our world certainly did not have the feel and taste of freedom. Unemployment and deprivation and the influence of the Catholic Church hung like a motionless cloud over the people. The heartbreak of immigration, the very bleak future for the person on the street were rarely spoken about; but existed in the hearts of the ordinary people. And my parents were ordinary people with extraordinary resolve and patience. My mother was busy from dawn to dusk looking after the seven of us, and her ability to handle a bob was legendry. My father was the most even tempered man you could meet, and went about his business without a murmur of protest. He worked with Houghton Timber Merchants in South Terrace as a delivery man, along with his faithful servant Peggy – Peggy Pony to give her correct title. Although she was called Peggy Pony I suspect that she was in fact a fully grown working horse. It was the era when the horse was still the principal means of transporting goods, and my father was proud to be let loose on the streets of Cork with Peggy Pony. He looked after that horse as if she had won the Grand National. Though Sunday was his only day off work, my father would go to the stables in South Terrace and bring Peggy up to our front garden. There was great excitement and fuss when our guest of honour would be paraded around. The children were taken on just one ride round the garden least Peggy would tire out – after all this was her only day of rest in a very busy schedule.

When the order was given that the horses were to be discontinued my father was heartbroken. I never found out what happened to

Peggy Pony afterwards, all I know is that my father was gloomy for weeks. My mother, who always took the responsibility for keeping the show on the road, had little time for sentiment and continually harped on to my father about taking more interest in the house and to forget the bloody pony. But I suppose that this was probably her only outlet for letting off steam; anyhow my father never took the slightest notice – he had the ability to turn off ever before switches were invented.

But eventually we did get too big for our place and we left to live in Friars Walk.

I was seven years old when we left the old house, and as we turned the corner at Crosses Green I looked back for the last time and shed a tear for 'The Mystery House.' The house that set fire to my imagination, and had frightened the living daylights out of me was gone from my life for all time.

If the Mystery House set fire to my imagination there was a house just across the road from us in Friars Walk that equally terrorised the children of the area. The house stood alone on the very edge of the park. When we arrived at our new home at Friars Walk there was a family living in the house, but rumours abounded, even at this early stage, that this was a strange house – even haunted. For whatever reason, the family did not stay too long and left without selling it. It looked more as if they abandoned the house, and to the amazement of the adults no one ever lived there afterwards, and eventually the house fell into disrepair. As no one had any interest in the house, the legion in the parish acquired the house and repaired it, put in facilities like table tennis and snooker and with some pomp and ceremony opened it up for the youth of the parish. Soon I was old enough to join the club and thus began my foray into the world of table tennis and snooker. We youngsters took to the games like ducks to water and pretty soon we had acquired a fair amount of skill, enough to feel that any of us could contest the world championships in either code. Joining the club had a price which we easily subscribed to, for most of us were gentle souls under the corduroy exteriors. We had to engage in the corporal works of mercy in the parish and had to attend rosary one night a week in the club, as we now called the house. One night, as we were saying the rosary in the house, accompanied by two or three adults we heard this ferocious banging on the door. Now the banging occurred on the inside door, and as the outer door was always locked it was a bit of a mystery how anyone could get in to the building. Immediately one of the adults who was kneeling just inside the door jumped up and opened the door. But to everyone's consternation, there was no one at the door. Having opened the door and seeing that no one was there, he rushed up the stairs and examined all the rooms, but not a sinner was found. At this stage we were all perplexed if not frightened but we resumed our prayers and carried on for another decade or two of the rosary. Suddenly we heard these great boots pounding on the stairs and as they came to the door, they gave it two almighty kicks that almost broke it in two. The door was opened immediately – not a single sign of a person. The front door was still heavily bolted and upstairs was as empty as ever. The whole saga was totally inexplicable; the rosary was abandoned for the night, as everyone, including the adults present, were scared out of their wits. I ran the twenty yards across the road to my house at Olympic pace. But the call of the snooker was strong and with the impetuosity of a youngster I again returned to the club with my friend. No sooner had we started and set up the balls on the table, when the boots started to trundle down the stairs again. We took off so fast that we did not even close the door. Many other people had the same experience as us, and when a blessing could not dislodge our friend with the hobnail boots, the house was closed down. But it was useful for another activity – hurling. It was great for honing our hurling skills playing against the wall of the house. It seems to me I spent my entire childhood lashing tennis balls against the side of that house to such an extent that I had perfected the art of hitting the same brick with uncanny accuracy. And the brick eventually fell out of the side of the house and I had discovered a new religion – hurling!

I am, who am!

Hurling was me and I was hurling. As I played more and more – I would not call it practice for there was not a scintilla of work involved – the better I got at it and the more my love grew for the sport. There was never the slightest doubt in my mind at any stage in my growing up, that one day I would not become an inter-county hurler for my beloved Cork. For obvious reasons I never related this to anyone at that stage, especially in Cork, where they have made the act of pulling people from high horses into an art form. The way I felt about hurling was unique, and I never felt this way about anything else in my life. It had nothing to do with cockiness; it had everything to do with knowing – in my heart, in my bones, in my soul.

And the learning skill was progressive – each year I was growing stronger and faster and acquiring new skills. Arriving at secondary school at Colaiste Chriost Rí just fuelled my passion even more and in no time I was on both hurling and football teams for the college. Somewhere in the recesses of my head I had thought that one day I would like to be a University Professor; the idea of being a teacher and imparting profound knowledge, while the same time delving into the great mysteries of love and death and birth seemed like an idyllic way to spend a life. But the tag on my head, to which I did not disagree was athlete, hurler and footballer – and not scholar.

And I got firmly implanted in that camp over my five happy years at school, and I left the bookwork to those better equipped to do it at that stage. To captain a senior hurling schools team at Colaiste Chriost Rí was a great honour, because generally it was accepted by your peers that you were most likely the best hurler on the team – so this honour meant a great deal to me. Also, being picked to wear the red jersey of Cork in all underage grades in hurling and football put me in the mix for a very successful seniors career. When I completed my leaving cert I went on a sabbatical to London for a year and this rest, away from all competition, only whetted my appetite for the sport when I returned. Add also the fact that I was improving my speed significantly each year, since I was fourteen, and when I resumed serious training I quickly became one of the top sprinters around.

With my natural skill and talent for hurling and my explosive speed – a lethal mixture for any sportsman – the future looked very rosy for the boy from The Mystery House.

No one could fuck it up but me!

And I did fuck it up.

I was playing at this stage for St. Finbarrs Hurling and Football Club and being a young rookie was after breaking into the senior teams. The senior hurling team had reached the final of the county championship and I had been an integral part of the team right to the final. At the pre-match meeting before the big game the team was announced and I was left off the team – only a sub. I could not believe my ears as I had played so well up to that – someone whispered in my young ear that one particular selector did not want me on the team. Being me I confronted him, he neither confirmed nor denied it, I flew into a rage and said I would not play again for the club when he was around. Because I was a sub that day I turned up for the match, came on in the second half of the match – however we were beaten, having been the overwhelming favourites. I threw back the jersey and bade farewell to hurling and to the greatest love of my life. It was a rush of blood to the head, by an immature and big-headed young fellow, and was easily the worst decision I have ever made in my life. Since I was three years old, I had been practicing and training for hurling, and just when I had broken through I abandoned the whole shebang just because of something really trivial. My father was devastated, and in his own gentle way tried to get me to go back and play again. But I had made my bed, and by Christ was I going to lie in it, such is the utter stupidity of youth. But the dye was cast and I had come to a fork in the road and I turned my back on hurling when I chose the other road. Sad to say, but I never took a hurley in my hand since that ill-fated day almost forty years ago.

But life tends to go on.

I was swaning around Fords at this time and had become a fully-fledged member of Leevale Athletic Club. While the mission statement for Leevale would proclaim that nurturing, developing and fostering athletics were the principal objectives of the club, the members might add an appendix – entertainment. At that time, before training methods and diet became serious issues, many of the members including myself, were in party-time mode and this we did, side-by-side with the athletics. Athletic sports days always culminated with plenty of booze and the compulsory sing–song. And Cork, being the sing-song capital of the world, we had more than our share of good entertainers. But in spite of all the partying, I had a lot of success on the track. But athletics was never my first love and therefore I never had the all-conquering approach to it that I had with the hurling.

And, as I began to clock up the years into my twenties, it looked very unlikely that my two dreams of becoming a famous hurler or scaling the heights of academia as a University Professor were ever going to be fulfilled. But in my case, God never closed one door, but he closed another as well.

CHAPTER THIRTEEN

It was the long summer weekend in London – the year was 1964. A shaggy-haired forty-something was preparing to leave his home for the weekend. He waved to his elderly mother, hopped on his twin cylinder 650 Triumph motorbike and headed down the Streatham High Road. With the sun on his back and the cooling breeze in his face he headed west. He hadn't the foggiest notion in the world where he was heading, but this was his normal modus operandi. Out of London he hit the A40 and headed in the direction of Wales. After one or two short stops he found himself on the Welsh border, and he figured that he would find a B&B for the night and sample some of the local ale. Suddenly, to his great surprise he came across a sign on the road which read Cork Ferry; Cork is where his late father was born. He himself was a born and bred cockney boy, and had never been to Ireland in his life, and all he knew about the place were the stories his father related to him over the years. But his father had been dead now for many a year, and the Irish interest had faded with his death. He followed the sign and sometime afterwards drew up to the ferry ship. Almost without thinking he bought his ticket on the spot and shortly afterwards found himself and his bike on the boat heading for Ireland. The last place on earth he thought he would be visiting that day when he set out from London. Arriving in Cork the following morning he smelt The River Lee for the first time, and as he headed into the centre of the city he gazed down on the pea-green river his father sang so passionately about for all those years. But he was like a balloon in the wind not knowing where he was going – he had some notion that he had some relatives in the city, for his father always spoke about Bella Heffernan or Bella Hanafin which was her married name. But that was a very long time ago and, if she was alive, she must be nearly a hundred.

Cork is a very confusing city for a stranger to find their way in, for just like the Seine in Paris, it has a north and south channel, and one never quite knows where they are in relation to the river. And this was exactly the story with Ronnie Heffernan. The one thing he was certain about was that she lived in Cork City. After some time driving around, he stopped at a house to ask some questions – the precise house was 14 Kyle St Cork City. He had stopped at the house of Bella Heffernan – mind boggling. And there she was setting in front of the fire still hale and hearty at ninety-four years old, and ready as only she could, to relate all the history and stories about his father – and how, when just a slip of a lad, he had joined the British Army, and like thousands of other Irish lads at the time, found himself at the front line in France. It was a re-union of kindred spirits and Ronnie spent the next three days riveted by this old woman with her magical stories, her knowledge of history and her love of music and song and her elephantine memory. And she would sing at the drop of a hat; morning, noon or night. For him, it was a spiritual homecoming and when the time came for him to rev up the bike once more, it was with a heavy heart that he bade her farewell. It was their first and only meeting for soon afterwards she took ill and died. But for Ronnie it was similar to the Star of Bethlehem story that guided him that day. The unbelievable coincidence of Ronnie pulling up outside the house, brought to mind another incredible coincidence, and strange enough it had a connection to my grandmother. It was the early sixties and my brother was playing for Cork in the Munster final in Thurles. Cork was playing Tipperary and there were over fifty thousand people at the match. I was but

- 161 -

a slip of a lad and was there with my father and my uncle having set out early from Cork City to get a sideline seat. We were seated next to this elderly gentleman and from his greeting we detected that he was an American. Sometime later my uncle remarked that the gentleman looked very much like my grandmother – eventually he could not contain his curiously any longer and passed a comment to the man that he had a great resemblance to his mother. Low and behold it transpired that the man's name was Billy Heffernan and he had been sixty years in America and he was a nephew of my grandmother. He had come to Ireland for a brief vacation and was returning from Shannon the following day.

Of all the gin joints …

When Ronnie had returned to London I kept in touch with him and, eventually it dawned on me after I completed my leaving cert, that it would be a nice little adventure to go to that city for a few months … the few months turned into a year and I can say it was the most exciting year in my life. If one had to choose any time to go to London, nineteen sixty-six would be top of the list. The city was heaving and the excitement and energy was palpable on the streets. It was a celebration of youth and I was not going to be left behind. I just loved London and Ronnie was the greatest tutor in the western world. The quiet spoken, unassuming man that I thought in my naivety to be just a gentle soul, turned out to be the most extraordinary man. He had done so many things and he was still only in his early forties – he was a writer, a painter, had a black belt for judo and karate, was a member of the anti-vivisection society of Great Britain, was a vegetarian and a great lover of animals. For the first time in my life I felt I met a true Christian, and it was strange for me to understand that in fact Ronnie did not believe in any religion. Coming from a country that professed to be, not alone Christian, but Catholic, meant that I was in for more than a shock in Pagan Britain. But my eyes were at last opening up to the world and seeing beyond the propaganda that had shaped my innocent mind up to then.

One of Ronnie's great friends was a man called George – and he was a complete contrast to Ronnie. One could safely say that he was the meanest man ever born; there was not even a contender within an ass's roar of him for absolute and unadulterated tightness. He owned a four story house in Mitcham and he kept lodgers for cash. He did everything for cash – his god was called Cash. He had been born a Jew but was converted to the God of Cash the very day he saw his first penny, and had remained true to his calling up to the time I laid eyes on him. He worked in the civil service in London and while his vocation was gathering money, his hobby was collecting degrees in the universities and third level institutions in that city. This man had more degrees than a compass – he said it was a fantastic way to meet loose women without costing him a dime. Though with George's legendary meanness, one could never imagine him buying a cup of tea for anyone at a rendezvous, never mind a drink. He had developed more tricks than Paul Daniels for avoiding paying for anything – one was to slip into the bar, order the drinks for his companions and then disappear into the jacks; and a battalion of the Gurkas could not get him out. Ronnie would get so pissed off with George that he would throw the money on the counter just for the sake of peace. Though I never drank alcohol in London, I would, out of honour, always pay for my round of drinks. This night I pulled an Irish sixpence from my pocket by mistake, George's eyes immediately recognized that it was a foreign coin, and when he admired it I gave it to him. A week or so later we were again in a pub, this time we had successfully corralled George into buying a round of drinks – he having imbibed from everyone else throughout the evening. With a scowl on his physiognomy he took the cash from his pocket; the barman being eagle-eyed and Irish asked George for the Irish sixpence, and there in front of the entire gallery, and without a hint of embarrassment he exchanged the Irish sixpence for an English sixpence. On the way home George made a comment about his economics teacher to the laughter of the mob.

"You mean that there is a human being in the world who is better at economics than yourself?" Ronnie gasped.

But it was the old story of the proverbial water falling off of the proverbial duck's back. By now our motley crew had grown to four having been joined on our outings by a friend from Cork. So, in order that we could travel together, Ronnie attached a wooden box to the motorbike. It was the most ridiculous sight in London – Ronnie driving, George on the back of the bike and Kevin and myself perched in the side box.

And we traveled everywhere!

To museums; to the theatre; to dances; to the coast.

What a life – education on wheels and fresh air.

But my few bob had run out and I needed to get a job, and like all young people, the crisis was upon me before I took some action. So I set out with a vengeance to get a job travelling from factory to factory until some bugger took pity on me and offered me a job. Eventually I got a job in a rubber factory, the hours being seven to seven – a long shift for a greenhorn like me who was not used to hard work. For some reason, Ronnie and his mother headed up to Birmingham for a week and the mother, being old and forgetful, never left a single item of food in the fridge. When I started this job I did not have a brass farthing to my name and all I could scrounge from the house was an apple for the day. After some initial training, by an ignorant little bastard on the factory floor, I was on my way and at least earning again. My job was to mould attachments to tubes in this bloody machine, and because I was the worst person since the beginning of time at anything that requires even the merest hint of manual dexterity, I was hopeless at this task. To be honest the scope of my manual dexterity just about stretched to shaving myself. The shaggin' tubes were coming out of the machine soft as ice cream, irrespective of how long I left the timer on. Add to this the fact that I was starved, famished, on death's door and a solitary apple was not about to solve that problem. The little fuckers working with me – all Maltese – were having the time of their lives, falling about the place with laughter, watching me making a complete horses ass of the job. Lunchtime came and we all disappeared to the canteen. They ordered roast beef, chicken, curry, and Yorkshire pudding, and I took out my miserable apple. At this juncture they were sure I was some kind of nutcase sitting down in front of an apple – I would have walked round the factory to escape the prying eyes of that lot if I had the energy, but I had been standing at this fecking machine and I was worn to a thread. With still half the day's shift to come, I still hadn't come to terms with the machine. And as if they had not eaten enough, the little bastards ordered deserts to chase down the dinner – I was suffering. Under my breath I cursed the bastards; I cursed myself for being so stupid for landing myself into this mess, and for having no way of getting any money for the rest of the week. I thought that unless I hit the free dinners in London, I could be returning to Ireland in a casket before the week was out. I stumbled through the afternoon attaining some degree of proficiency at the machine, which meant that I had a job for the following morning, providing I had the energy to rise from the bed. At finishing time I was the weariest human being in Britain trudging my way home to a long drink of Adams Ale and straight into the scratcher. Mercifully, the fatigue took command and I fell into a deep sleep, only to wake and remember that I had to face Belsen once more. I dragged myself to the factory and started on the machine hoping that I would fall down dead on the floor. But I had no such luck and the bastards were still chirping away at me in the background. The day wore on but without the luxury of any apple that day. By now my ribcage was coming inwards and touching my backbone, and the ring on my finger was gradually working itself loose. Christ I though, I'll be a walking skeleton before payday. The idea of selling my body for a few quid was gaining prominence in my head, but I would have to move pretty smartly for shortly there would be nothing left to sell. I was fading away at the rate of knots.

Going downhill badly.

I was so bad on the third day, that I was envious of the factory cat who had scavenged the head of a sardine and was eating it right in front on my eyes. What I would give now for a lump of sardine – with or without his head – tucked away in a fresh crusty roll. But the bad thought; like thinking about food is not good for one. Put my mind on the job – get those fucking moulds working – suffocate the senses with the piecing smell of rubber and erase the images of the bastards tucking into sirloin steak and chips and onion rings on the side. By now I felt that I was falling out of my shoes as well – and all traces of a stomach had by now disappeared from the radar screen. How I made it home that evening will be the topic of many a PhD thesis in the future. Suffice to say, that I reached my pad in a hallucinatory condition, drank my customary glass of water and threw myself on the bed and prayed that I would not wake up.

Thursday was a replica on Wednesday, with added suffering.

But time and the hour runs through the roughest day and Friday came round, and I could not be any happier if I had won the

Littlewoods Pools when I saw that that sun rising. Perhaps I could write to the Prime Minister of Britain and put myself forward for the Victoria Cross – this kind of heroism was rarely seen in Britain in the sixties. Somehow I didn't feel hungry any more – with the impending wage packet only hours away.

Was my body telling me something?

Perhaps I would drop down dead on the floor if I bit into a rock salmon. Maybe I should report to Balham General Hospital and go on the drip for a few days in order to prepare my body for food again.

But I need not have worried.

At the first sight of the pay packet my hunger returned with a vengeance. Dead on one o'clock, just on the sound of the siren I shot up to the canteen, much to the consternation of the bastards, for they were under the impression that I was some kind of religious freak who was mortifying his body like some kind of ancient Irish monastic settler. On reaching the canteen I slowly opened the pay packet and ran my fingers over the crispy notes – is it any wonder, in the wide world, that people kill for this stuff?

I looked at the overhead menu and my eyes feasted on the fare available that day. The voice rang out from behind the counter

"Are you going to look at the menu for the rest of the day mate?"

"I'll just have the fresh cod and chips … and peas … and two savory pies … and a few sausages … and bread and butter," I added in.

"Christ Paddy, is there a famine on the way?"

I forced a smile.

"And a pot of tea."

He shoveled the food onto the plate, and I disappeared into the corner to devour the grub – bit-by-bit by delicious-bit. I thought of old Mr. Shaw again when he remarked that the only true love was the love of food. The old adage also came to mind that more people die from food than famine, so I took my time relishing every delicious mouthful. I brought to mind the stories I had heard about the hunger strikers of 1916 –22 periods and how many of them had died when they resumed eating. Heroically I had made it so far – I did not want to fall at the final hurdle. But life is full of unforeseen hurdles. The bastards had returned to the factory floor before me and had stolen my entire mornings work – they had collected all the moulds that I had made and distributed them between themselves. Our wages were made up of piecework and the biggest bonuses went to those who produced the most. Seeing what happened I returned to the factory floor and asked in a polite manner as to who had stolen my work. They flashed their sparkling white teeth at me in total ridicule. But they did not know that they were dealing with a descendant of a Fenian leader in Cork, and a descendent of a great-grandmother that almost bit off the finger of a British army captain when he was searching her house, or that my uncle and his friend broke the scales of justice on the roof of the courthouse in Cork. Calmly I walked straight over to the leader of the pack, grabbed him with both hands under his Adam's apple.

"Now if my work is not returned in one minute I'm going to choke this little fucker here."

That knocked the Maltese shit out of them, and as fast as their feet could carry them they had the moulds back in their rightful spot in seconds.

By this stage the leader of the pack was shaking like a leaf and his tongue was stuck to his palette with absolute fear. I pushed him clear and walked to my bench and resumed work, much to the consternation of the confused mob.

One of the mob ran to the foreman's office shouting that "Paddy gone mad."

Not long afterwards the security brought me up to the Managing Director's Office. This was a serious offence. The Managing Director sat me down and in a very British tone asked me to explain myself. I gave him chapter and verse, and when I had finished he smiled in my direction.

"Listen," he said, "I'm from Tipperary and I know all about those geezers – came over here myself over thirty years ago now ... I know their game," I pointed out that he sounded more British than the British themselves.

"It creeps up on you over the years without being aware of it, look let me transfer you to a different area away from the trouble, perhaps into the office."

I thanked him, told him I was just on an extended holiday and was returning to college in Cork and I would prefer to cut and run at this stage.

"Cork," he uttered.

"Never lost it for causing trouble ... I'll forward on your stuff."

"It's not easy being a rebel."

I shook his hand and gathered my few things, and left the factory and the miserable bastards and the pungent smell of the rubber far behind.

Out once more on the streets of London; the cars whizzing by, the acrid smell of the pollution hanging in the watery sunshine, and my pay packet firmly secured in my pocket. And my first real lesson, in London living, well and truly learned.

More job hunting for Monday morning – at least with food in the belly.

The odd couple – Ronnie and his mother returned over the weekend but I held my council about the events that had shaped my week.

"I managed great with the cooking, yeah, but I retired from my job."

This rash behaviour appealed to Ronnie, but his mother cast a jaundiced eye in my direction.

She still could not get a handle on this innocent faced Irish lad with the funny voice that had dropped from the sky into her house. She was a Conservative with a capital C, and this is where the great dilemma of her life manifested itself – how did she produce a chap like Ronnie?

But the apple does not fall too far from the tree, and knowing the stories about Ronnie's father which my grandmother had related; it was not surprising that Ronnie was always predestined to be a Bohemian. When I eventually related the true story about the job to Ronnie and my attempted 'murder' on the leader of the pack my standing shot up many notches in his eyes.

But London in the sixties was the land of opportunity and quickly I picked up another job making alternators. I was the only man on the island, so to speak – I was working with a crew of twelve Jamaican women ranging from eighteen to eighty.

And were they fun!

Bear in mind that I had come from the most Catholic and conservative country on the planet, and that the thunderous roar of the Passionists Fathers could still be heard the length and breadth of the country, it was totally astounding for me to be lopped into the midst of this bunch of free and liberal females. I was only in the door when the request came that Miranda wanted to sleep with me – I could have shit myself on the spot. At this stage in my life I was a virgin to the power of ten, in fact if the opportunity was given to me on the proverbial plate I would run a country mile with fear. But like a good Irish catholic boy who did not drink or sleep around, I put all these bad thoughts to one side as I got on with the job of making a few bob – London was a big place and I needed the spondulux to explore and enjoy the adventure – and it was a fantastic adventure travelling here, there, and yonder in the side box of Ronnie's bike. When we would scurry round Piccadilly Circus or Whitehall, it was great to see the faces of the onlookers smiling at this contraption, carrying two young lads and two seasoned old geezers. We could have been part of the Carry on Brigade.

One of the big nights in London or any part of the world in the Irish calendar is of course Patrick's Day. George and Ronnie were frequent visitors to the cheese and wine parties at the Fairfield Halls in Croydon, and when the notice went up for that year that a special night was planned again for St Patrick's Night the duo were jubilant. They knew from previous nights that the place would be packed to the rafters with Irish nurses. Maybe, just maybe, they could use the two young bucks – Kevin and myself – to net some of these beauties. They were fed up to the teeth with the stuffy old ones at the cheese and wine parties, and also there was a little matter which had not escaped George that the entire evening was free – even the booze. The 650 Triumph Thunderbird with the wooden box was our preferred mode of transport for the evening and we duly jumped aboard. That should really impress the nurses.

The atmosphere at the party was fantastic and green was the order of the day – green dresses, green hats and scarves, and badges and shamrock to beat the band. And of course, the place was packed with nurses from every corner of Ireland. The old ones from the cheese and wine gatherings were present also, but by nifty footwork, the Two Randys managed to stay clear of them. Ronnie had his usual pint in tow, while Monsieur George had a large brandy in his glass which he diligently kept topped-up throughout the evening. George, now well on the way to being merry, introduced this young girl to me – he had engaged her in conversation and asked her to dance but she declined, so he did the next best thing and introduced her to me. She wore the shortest skirt I had ever seen, and was as flirtatious as a filly. Both her parents were Irish and she was as crazy as a March hare. When you danced with Lisa you got involved in a contest that almost ended up in the accident and emergency. She gripped so hard you could feel every contour of her lean body, so much so, that for a garsun like me it was something akin to an out-of-body experience.

And she came home with the gang, and if the contraption looked funny arriving earlier on, it looked positively hilarious now with the terrible five in transit. Lisa sat between Kevin and myself, her bare legs and thighs exposed for the whole world to have a look. Embarrassment is the one word you would not find in her dictionary, but she was a fun, liberated girl, who had embraced the emerging new culture and spirit of London. We dropped her off somewhere along the way and she disappeared into the night never to be encountered by us again. We made many expeditions in and around London on the bike, but now I was harboring ideas of my own. I got ambitions to drive a bike myself and soon I was viewing a 500 Gold Flash BSA at the second hand motorbike shop.

Did I want this beautiful shiny God!

The cash price was out of my league for a trainee alternator worker so the big man came to my rescue and came up with the extra cash.

"You have all your life to pay me back," said Ronnie

And of course the great man had to ride the 500 BSA Gold Flash back to the house for me, for I had never driven a bike in my life. I managed to pay for the insurance and license myself, and in no time was ready for the road. And in spite of myself, I managed to get good at the work of assembling alternators, and the women at the job took me to their bosom – in a metaphorical sense – and I earned a lot of dough to be spent on the highways and byways of Britain. The team now traveled in convoy – well two vehicles! Ronnie and his faithful crew of George and Kevin (in the box) and myself now riding solo on my shiny Gold Flash, exploring the museums, the castles and the old mansions and the beaches – we could have been the founding fathers of The Antique Roadshow. At last my education had begun, for as WB once remarked that, education was not only imparting knowledge but lighting a fire – I lit a fire in 1966 and it has not gone out since. And thus the wonderful summer of adventures was coming to an end and I started to make arrangements to return to Ireland in the autumn. When the time eventually came to say goodbye to Mitcham Lane, and The Locarno Dancehall, and the claustrophobic cheese and wine parties in the Fairfield Halls, and to Old London itself, it was with a heavy heart that I said farewell. But the crew wanted to accompany me to Fishguard and so they assembled for the last time – same combination – and we all headed west. On reaching Fishguard, Ronnie decided there and then, that he would join me and travel to Ireland. George decided to return to London by train. George boarded the ship with us to say a last goodbye, but suddenly realising that he was now on board and there was no check on tickets, and he could safely travel to Ireland without paying, was enough to sway him to come along as well. The ship sounded her horn and we were on our ten hour journey to Cork. My mother was all a fuss when she saw the Terrible Two that I had brought home with me. Of course she was acquainted with Ronnie from his earlier visit but George was a different kettle of fish – he was not a relative, he was a stranger so he needed extra attention.

It was by the Banks of the Lee that Ronnie fell in love – with Murphy's Stout!

Hook, line and sinker.

He fell head over heels in love with the creamy stuff. He never turned down an opportunity to go to the boozer and always had me in tow, even though I had never tasted the black stuff or any stuff for that matter. George kept my family in raptures with his stories of fighting in Asia and his many adventures in the forests of Borneo. Outside our house in Friars Walk became the most famous landmark in Cork – teams of teenagers made the pilgrimage from all parts of the city to view the monster parked outside. The shiny, silver frame, against the black background on the bike, and that massive twin exhausts stretching under the bike just oozed power. The box attached to the sides lent a sense of hilarity to the scene, as they tried to figure what in God's name it was doing attached to the bike. But while the pilgrims were admiring the 650 Triumph Thunderbird, the Terrible Two were on hot pursuit of Murphy's Stout in every street in Cork. They were in Cork just for four days but they were determined to visit every watering station within the four walls of the city.

And I was their guide.

Early start and we are in the first bar by five o'clock and working our way on this particular pub crawl up Oliver Plunket Street, downing the mandatory pint of Murphy's at each venue. By eight o'clock and six pints later we are firmly ensconced in the music bar and George is getting very excited at the sight of the 'Young Ladies.' The same again. By now the rock shandies – lemonade and orange mixed – are almost pouring out of my nose and The bold George now firmly fortified with the drink disappears from the scene only to return with a 'young lady' hanging off his arm. Now by any stretch of the imagination the middle-aged war veteran could be considered attractive – his deep set slanty eyes, his dark tangled skin, and a pair of ears that were made for supporting glasses. But beauty is, as beauty does, and he had pulled a bird less than half his age and he was scowling like the Cheshire cat. He told her he was a talent scout over from Britain and that he was seeking out attractive Irish girls with good voices to offer them a career in the music business. When he asked her what she would like to drink, she replied that a brandy and ginger ale would be fine. That did it. He headed towards the counter and slipped out the side door – every man has his breaking point. When she realised that the talent scout was not returning, she stood up and muttered to us that he was nothing but an old wanker and she quickly departed the scene. Soon afterwards, as we attempted to finish our drinks and try and locate the lost one, another girl approached us.

"Do you know the girl you were just talking to … be careful of her … she's an Elizabethan"

In Cork the word Lesbian had not entered the lexicon yet.

It was time for departure for the bold travellers and they poured onto the Innisfallen on the Friday night, and they sailed away down the river into Cork harbour and out into the wide ocean, and they went out of our lives.

And we never set eyes on them again.

I maintained contact with Ronnie for some time but the letters seem to disappear into the ether and soon all contact was lost.

CHAPTER FOURTEEN

I got a present for my sixtieth birthday.

Neuropathy.

Up to this, my place on the all-time list for contracting illness's might have been in doubt having had only gout, peptic ulcer, broken ankle, liver failure, eye migraine, four operations on my hands and feet and open heart surgery. I was hospitalized on ten occasions and I attended out-patients clinics and appointments with doctors, ten thousand times and gave one hundred thousand pints of blood for analysis. My medical team consisted of the following: general practitioner, cardiologist, rheumatologist, nephrologist and I had now co-opted a newcomer to my stable – neurologist. Now throw into the mix my medication requirements – zocor, cozaar, nu-seal, celebrex, emcor, neurontin, colchicine, one-alpha, zyloric, and B complex.

And after all that I get neuropathy for my birthday.

It was like throwing a bag of coal on to the top weighted horse in the Grand National just as he is heading out to complete the four and a half mile run.

Nowadays, when most people are approaching sixty, they are planning a trip on the Orient Express or planning a boating trip up the Amazon – I was heading to the Mount Carmel Hospital with my pajamas under my oxter ready for a lumber puncture. And this bloody neuropathy started so innocently – just a little uncomfortable feeling in my legs when I hit the sack at bedtime. But from a humble beginning it grew into a total menace in a very short time. I had never heard of neuropathy or any kind 'opathy' in my life up to that point, but I sure knew about it now – for I found it impossible to sleep at night. It is as if your feet have suddenly got a life, all of their own, and an engine is constantly humming away causing those awful creeping sensations. Along with the sensations comes a deadening of the nerves in the feet causing a numbness which in itself is quite alarming. This was all diagnosed in hospital and the name firmly nailed to it, caused, if you don't mind, by the colchicines – a medication which I had been taking to dampen down the gout. While the neurologist was crossing all his T's, dotting all his I's and filling out the lorry load of papers to attach to an already massive tome – my medical file, I quietly suggested that he bury it in the college of surgeons, as some kind of medical history record of the diseases suffered by an inhabitant of the twentieth and twenty first century – they were all there in alphabetical order.

But he held his Hippocratic line and suggested that from now on I should concentrate on the positives in my life – like that I was still alive, I was about to mutter. A little bit of lateral thinking never goes astray and we must always be endeavoring to get new perspectives in this ever-changing world of ours. This put me in mind of my son when he was about six years old. My wife had a habit of buying dinkies every week for him, to such an extent that he had hundreds of the cars. Favourite among these dinkies was a yellow Volkswagen beetle which he played with incessantly. One day, while driving down the Belgard, we were passed by a yellow Volkswagen beetle and my son, quick as a flash, called out, "hi Da, look at the man driving the big dinky." Lateral Thinking. Thinking outside the box. Get in touch with Anthony Robbins again – now he'd be a good man to start with, and mention to him that I'm about to leave hospital for the umpteenth time and I am physically and mentally fucked. Just before I departed the hospital, the Filipino nurse dropped another atomic bomb: she said that I was colour blind – it was clear as day on my chart. Jesus, how many more diagnoses have they made, and they're not even telling me about them at this stage.

"Here," I said to the nurse, "is there any mention of Bird Flu or The Black Plague on my chart?"

"Now I think you have enough to be getting on with for the moment," she smiled a wonderful open smile and just as she was tucking the sheets in at the end of the bed she looked in my direction and asked her question.

"Mr. Archer, what is it like seeing the world in black and white?"

I was flummoxed ...

"Don't have an idea in the world how to answer that, I never even knew I was color blind in the first place."

She skipped out of the ward and just as she was rounding the door popped her head back, and in her enchanting way, suggested that I think about it and to let her know if I thought of an answer. But I never did think of an answer and when I was released from the hospital out onto the streets I pondered how in God's name I was going to cope with this nasty neuropathy on top of all the other bloody ailments. Color blindness was never going to be top of my list.

But where do I go from here?

Quo vadis, indeed?

I had successfully come through the open heart surgery and got myself back to a good fitness level over the months. That old enemy – post operative stress disorder – popped up his head from time to time, but being on guard, following warnings from the rehab people, meant that one was forewarned. But I was down in the dumps again before I realised it. This was principally due to the fact that I found it almost impossible to sleep at night; therefore, I was totally shagged out in the morning. The little bugger called depression was making inroads in a very sinister manner. Being sixty was leaving its mark, and when I was endeavoring to pluck up the courage and enthusiasm to extradite myself from the morass the words of the doctor were floating round in my head. Always be looking for new perspectives.

Did I get it from Mr. Robbins? Not on your nanny.

I got it from a pair of new air shoes I bought in the sale. When I opened them up in the morning to fling my tired feet into them, there it was staring up at me. Printed on the inside sole were the immortal lines:

Never, ever give up trying!

It struck a cord somewhere deep inside me. I conjured up images of the Mystery House where I first saw the light of day on the banks of the Lee, and how my parents strove to always do their very best for us, I thought of my grandparents and the rough world they were born into – the seed of hope again was growing stronger inside my head and my resolve was growing that this fucking thing was not going to defeat me. The hidden emotion in my bones was coming to the surface and making me stronger. The afternoon would see me back in the park striding out and I was making plans for the comeback to beat all comebacks. My wife suggested I get in touch with a life coach – she read in one of the Sunday Magazines that they were the greatest things since the birth of the sliced pan. She said that a sixty year old man might need a bit of direction, having hit that great milestone, and especially someone with a dodgy pedigree in the mental stakes. Basically she was saying, that a lunatic like me needed some guidance and, with my new found zeal, I was about to take her up on the advice.

The golden page was dragged out – life coaches were the section I was scanning.

I selected a man with a baldy head; in this way I thought that I would have instant empathy – but I got suspicious when he said he would call out to meet me in my house. But he had a landline telephone number listed along with his mobile number and that instilled some confidence so I took the chance. I noted the appointment in my black diary. Christ what if he turns out to be a serial killer and after all the vicissitudes I have endured in my life to be choked to death in my own home. I suggested to my wife that she be present when he came out to our house, but she said it was just my anxiety neurosis coming to the fore once again. When I rang him back to change to a time when my wife might be at hand, in case I needed instant attention, he said it would be better for me to be alone at our first meeting. This convinced me, more than ever, that I would not see the light of day again following his visit. Counting down the days to Mr. Sigel's visit – the life coach – was defeating the whole purpose because I had promised myself to be more positive.

The big day dawned and the Merc arrived outside the door. Out from the car stepped the skinniest man walking on the northern hemisphere and approached my door. He did not even make a foot tap, for the dog was as silent as a mouse – never heard a thing. I opened the door for him and in my anxiety asked if he was the coach or the taxi. He gave a watery smile, put his hand out in my direction to be clasped and pushed his briefcase in before him through the door. I ushered him to the torture chamber, he sat down, and I sat down, and we viewed each other from afar, not sure who was the one that needed the help. And now for the pleasantries, yes this was a lovely day but there might be rain in the wind – the Cork breaking out in me again because I'm in that awkward state. He said his name was Michael.

"So Mr. Archer ... Jim, it was nice of you to see me today, I hope that I can be of help to you."

"Well my wife was the instigator of this meeting, I would never have dreamt of seeking a life coach to help me."

"Well here I am, willing and I trust able to be of immense help."

His thin hands now dangled puppet-like.

"Firstly, I would like you to fill out this questionnaire – it should take about ten minutes, and we both will find it helpful to establish a programme for you."

He drew a folder from his briefcase.

"In the meantime, I have some stuff I want to get on with here."

He smiled, as if to tell me to shag off – and I did shag off – to the kitchen.

My work completed, my medical history and the state of my mind documented I returned to the Guru. By now he had donned a pair of glasses with half lenses and was viewing me over the top part of the lenses as if I were an exhibit at the Natural History Museum. And worse was to unfold, when he began to read the questionnaire. If the face is the mirror of the soul, this man was quickly arriving at the conclusion that he was dealing with the biggest wanker this side of the equator.

"Are you seriously telling me that you have all those medical conditions?"

"Every one of them," I said kind of half boasting.

He began to gather his papers, and he raised his head to look in my direction. He gave a sigh and half looked in my direction once more.

"Who do you think I am – Padre Pio? Book a trip to Lourdes … or better still Medjagoria."

He headed for the door like a man out of control repeating under his breath … these bastards are looking for miracle workers … miracle workers they want.

He beat a hasty retreat down the pathway and he could not get to his car fast enough.

I stood rooted to the spot … I was flummoxed …

What did I do to cause all this?

Now I was back to square one, but I realized, and it was certainly consoling, that there were other people worse off than myself – life coaches!

Well good riddance to him – he was gone out of my life and I still had the grand bank draft in my sweaty little paw.

I retired to my little corner of the room and crunched up on the old sofa. Then my eureka moment came to me! Look I'm sixty – I lived a bit and learned a bit, I probably know twice as much as the twit who calls himself a life coach. The answer to my depression was to communicate with the outside world again. I could put lateral thinking to the test. Perhaps I could become a political adviser, well not one that would be trailing ministers round the Dail like some kind of lapdog, but an adviser working from the confines of the home – a far more honorable and prestigious occupation. I decided to cook an extra special meal for the wife and myself, and then to spring my new idea on her when she's just about to sip the Bailey's Cream. Out with the French cookery book – Boeuf Bourguignonne – now there's an idea!

With my apron firmly in place, and the beef and the red wine rearing to go, I launched into my task. I gathered the olive oil, the thyme, celery, carrots, flour, tomatoes and the mushrooms onto the kitchen worktop for preparation and, in no time, had my oven on the run and the first step of my scheme in place.

Whatever she expected when she came home I am not sure, but one thing was she did not expect to see, was me all decked out in an apron and bottles of red and white wine on the table.

"What happened with the life coach – you did not answer your phone all day?"

"Ah, him, he was only an old bollocks."

"Sure no one could get on with him." I told her the story as it had happened that day.

"And what's with the wine and all the razzamatazz?"

"Just a little celebration because it's Tuesday," I gently put it.

"Do you know you are going more bonkers by the day, I don't know if it has anything to do with the neuropathy."

I stretched out my hand and poured her a nice Ricard, to prepare the body for what was coming next on the menu.

"Where the hell did you get this stuff … haven't seen it in years. There's something up!"

"For God's sake, drink up and sit yourself down there."

We had a little smoked fish and brown bread starter and a glass or two of Chateauneuf du Pape and I introduced the main gig of the evening – the Boeuf Bourguignonne. This went down a treat and soon I introduced the fromage and another glass or two of the vin and we were ready for the coffee and the Bailey's Cream and the little announcement of the evening.

"You're going to do what? Become a political adviser … What do you know about politics?"

"Not a lot, I must admit but that's not the point ... I know a lot about life ... I know a lot about illness and doctors and medication and walking in the park ... what I'm trying to say is that I know a lot about human nature – and politics is about dealing with human nature."

"Is this the lateral thinking malarkey?"

"Something like that," I said, for the sake of peace.

"We'll talk about it another time. Drink up that drop of Bailey's and I'll get you another."

Just before we put out the light that night she turned to me and asked, "And what did you call that meal we had tonight?"

"Boeuf Bourguignonne," I replied.

"Sure, there's no end to your talent."

"Do you mean political or culinary?"

"Forget it you eejit, go to sleep."

That night, I dreamt of the life coach Sigel as he emerged from a graveyard, hands all dangling, eyes missing and heading straight for me. I leapt up in the bed as if I was doing the Fosbury Flop and almost dislocated my shoulder. The wife, thinking I was getting a heart attack, immediately jumped out of bed and started ringing the ambulance services – but I stopped her, just in time.

"That's the last time you're drinking Bailey's in this house, it drives you barmy."

I settled down to sleep this time: thankfully without a visit from you know who, and the birds were greeting me from my back garden when I woke from my slumbers.

And this was another day of the rest of my life.

The Political Phase.

That sounded very important, like … The Thirty Years War.

It had a nice ring to it.

I wonder does the Taoiseach know about lateral thinking. Maybe I'll just drop him a line and make a few suggestions.

"Listen," said the wife "if you're going to write to the Taoiseach of this country making a complete idiot of yourself, you might as well pack your bags and get out of this house, I have put up with madcap ideas for far too long it's about time you grew up."

"Does this mean that my political career is over before it began?"

"Precisely that, now get out of my way I have work to attend to."

Being sixty is not fun, but as my pharmacist said to me on that auspicious day, there is only one thing worse than reaching sixty – and that is not reaching sixty. I was still trying to be upbeat and follow the philosophy of the air-shoe to never give up, but there were days when I was losing the battle. Perhaps my mid-life crisis had been delayed by all the medication I had taken over all those years.

The next morning the wife comes up with a suggestion.

"I've been thinking during the night, and do you know what you want?"

Christ, I didn't have the foggiest what was going to spill out of her mouth.

"I've been thinking, and I have come to the conclusion, that you are suffering from house fatigue."

"What, in the name of all that's holy, is house fatigue?"

"House fatigue is a common disease mostly suffered by housewives from being stuck in the house all day every day, what you need is a change of atmosphere."

I started thinking, maybe she's going to try and get me committed, and after all, I have been acting strange since the birthday. But her thinking was more humane than I anticipated.

"You need a trip away from the home scene; a few days in the west of Ireland would do you no harm. I'll get your few things together later on in the day and you can head off in the morning."

She was in some hurry to pack me off.

But I did not complain. It was years since I went anywhere on my own and I looked forward to the open road and the promise of a nice hotel, a good meal and a walk by the seashore – yes that should go a long way to restoring my equilibrium. I hit the shower at first light and suddenly realised that I was whistling for the first time in ages. A little boy (of sixty), looking forward to his first outing on his own for yonks. With a bulging wallet, I was well armed as I headed out the M50, and soon I was waving goodbye to dirty old Dublin. Even the legs felt better – maybe I should be doing this on a regular basis. The sun was up; I flung open the two windows of the car to let the cool breeze on my face, put on radio 2 for the first time in decades (it had even changed its name unbeknown to me) and let it all hang out so to speak.

I could have been a youngster again if I could only turn back the clock, but alas, time had already brought me down the alleyway and beat the shit out of me. But this day was not a day to reflect on time, or ageing, or death. It was time to grab life by the belly and enjoy the moment. It felt good to be alive – very good indeed. Towards late afternoon, I arrived in Westport with a sore ass from driving, but a sense of adventure in my bones and a thirst that would take some quenching – but I was in the right watering hole.

"Are you Golden?" said the receptionist.

"Am I what?"

"Are you with the Golden Breaks Brigade?"

"Jes, I've heard of the Irish Brigade, but I never heard of the Golden Brigade."

She laughed.

"Well they are due here today."

I was thinking the Zimmer Brigade, but I was now one of them myself, so I better be careful.

"So would you prefer to pay the full lash or will I put you in with the mob?"

"If I can save money you could put me in with the Mafia."

I became the latest recruit for the Golden Brigade – and I got a huge discount and a list of events for the next three days that would test an Olympic Marathon man. As soon as I reached my spacious room, I got on the mobile to the wife to tell her she was married to the latest member of the Golden Brigade. That would go down like a hole in the head.

"Have you any pride in the world?" she muttered, "joining in with a load of … well, old age pensioners."

"But I got a forty per cent discount."

She was not impressed; she was feeling old, by implication.

"The next time I'll try to align myself with a bunch of models."

"It might be no harm, that might see the end of you," she was not holding back her punches.

The banter over, I could get down to the real business of the day – sleep.

I was knackered after the long drive and I needed a kip to recover. After all, the evening promised hectic antics for the night the – forty-five-card game. I threw myself on the bed, gazed out at the ever-changing colours of the western sky and soon I was fast asleep – as befits a Golden Brigade man in the late afternoon. I woke to the stillness just as the first shade of darkness was invading the room and casting strange shadows on the wall.

I felt strange myself.

The mind began to wonder, but before it took root I upped from the warm bed, headed for the bathroom and douched myself with the soft warm water of Mayo, followed by the coldest shower dumped on any human being in the west that day. I better dress well to impress this lot tonight – my chances might be good.

There is something odd about a bunch of old geezers together – it reminds me of a large churn of soft chocolate – I find it very off-putting. Perhaps it's a kickback to my youth when my mother and myself would visit my grandfather at St. Finbarrs Hospital. It somehow made me profoundly sad to see so many old people just lying in beds ready to pass on to the next life. I never wanted to get old, and here I was myself in Westport, a fully fletched member of the Golden Oldies.

But I was not about to go quietly into the night.

Firstly I had to turn this lot inside out, upside down, for the fun that's in them and there was plenty.

"A double Pernod there, garcon."

I was in full swing at the bar, the blue rinse chicks watching my every move.

If the wife could only see me now, she would realise the charismatic man she had married.

"Give the ladies another drink on me."

I was winning hands down, much to the annoyance of some fellow males, who could only gaze and admire a true professional at work.

Another bottle or two of plonk at the dinner and I was glittering.

Never got to the 45 card game though – had to be taken upstairs to bed by the two porters after getting sick all over the blue rinse ladies.

Tres gallant!

I woke with the father and mother of a head. The mobile was hopping like a demented rat on the bed next to me – soon the wife was screeching down the line like a fish woman; she was sure something had happened to me when she could not get in touch. Bleary-eyed I glanced at my watch – Christ it was three o'clock.

I assured my wife that I was still in the land of the living, just, and that I had mislaid my mobile at the card game.

"Everything is grand, couldn't be better, speak to you later."

She was still angry, but assured when she hung up.

"Oh my shaggin' head."

Little pictures were filtering through what was once considered a brain, and it did not make for easy viewing. Getting sick all over that fucking bunch – it could not be worse if I threw up on the Little Sisters of the Poor Clares.

It was the males in the ranks of The Golden Brigade who took most offence, but being the cowards they were, they never mentioned it to me. But I could see it everywhere in their eyes.

"Arsehole," their eyes uttered, when I passed by.

The females were more forgiving. Raising families prepared them for all sorts of disasters and mine was a disaster. When the security of the hotel marched me into the manager's office, and after he had thrown the red card at me and warned me to vacate the premises within the hour, it was the Blue Rinse commandos that came to my rescue.

'One out, all out,' this was fighting talk.

Hannibal himself would not stand up to this lot, so the manager capitulated and I got a reprieve. I promised myself to stay clear of double pernods in the future.

The best cure for a hangover, I was once informed, was a sauna – so I grabbed my togs and towel and headed south to the leisure centre. By this time, a fair collection of the Brigade had assembled poolside, and they were a sight to behold. The women were all lumpy and full of brown spots, the men, sporting scars across their chests – signifying to all and sundry, that they had been under the knife. It was like a right-of-passage to old age by the men. Some of them, especially the baldy ones, had grown forests of hair on their chests and this acted as a barrier for the scars to the peering eyes of the nosey. I felt right at home, as I had all the necessary tee shirts and badges.

'Jes, but it's still awful to be getting old.'

And you feel so helpless!

So it was the sauna for me, to sweat out the shit from the system. A group of us sat silently in the sauna, occasionally glancing to get a sneaky look at the person opposite, to see if they were still alive. The quietness was deafening – we just sat there like a bunch of old timers, waiting for the daily delivery of the meals-on-wheels. The heat of the sauna was beginning to work; the haze was lifting from my eyes and I kind of felt half-human again. At this rate of progress I could be hitting the pool before the Bovril is served – this was a must on the afternoon menu, I was assured. While some would settle for a cup of tea and a Marietta, the majority would get irate if they had not had the cup of Bovril to sustain them 'til dinner at eight. God only knows what they would demand if they were paying anything substantial for their stay at the hotel. Here was I, one of the foot soldiers of The Golden Brigade, but there was something deep inside me that would not allow me to think of myself as one of them. A swim could banish a few thoughts from my head and have me fit and well for the anticipated excitement of the night – the bingo.

Now there is something, to keep the Alzheimer's at bay.

I had come to Westport to clear my head and now I was resorting to the cynical me once more. At dinner I did my best to avoid the ladies, but not as much as they did to avoid me – so I sat next to Jack with the red nose. If my calculation was correct, and if I was any reader of human nature, or indeed physiognomy, Jack would have cargo on board and therefore might be more tolerant to the frailties of a man like myself. My judgement was correct – Jack was spiffo. The damage was done upstairs – drank a half bottle of Paddy ever before he hit the dining room. Another few glass of vino and we could have a repeat performance, only this time, it would be Jack who would take the leading role. For this reason, I removed myself to a safer place at the table – but I need not have bothered, Jack could consume Lough Corrib and it would hardly cause a stagger.

Isn't it amazing the gifts we are born with!

My mobile hops again – this time it's the wife – it had to be the wife, for I have never got a call from anyone else.

"And how is the House Husband on tour?"

She's in sparkling form now – this holiday is doing her more good than me.

"Great ... just digging into the grilled salmon."

"And how are the ravers?"

This sarcasm is a new trait I have not noticed before.

"Bursting and rearing to go, 'tis hard for a man to keep his underpants on down here."

I got a few shocked looks from the table opposite.

"The neuropathy is not acting up then?"

"Sure it did not have a chance to show itself," I replied.

"Look, the salmon will be after swimming back to sea if I don't get a hold of him, I'll ring you tomorrow."

The looks from the other tables were very telling.

I hit the jackpot at the bingo. The youngest, and by far the best-looking member of the Brigade, sat next to me at the game.

"You look like an interesting guy to me," she whispered in my ear.

"And how's that I replied?" knowing the evil ways of women on vacation.

"You just have that, je ne sais quoi, about you," she replied, this time with a far huskier voice.

Jes, I was getting worried now.

Having arrived at the hotel with two bags – one for my clothes and the other for my medication, a man would be worried about getting excited like that. It might be just my luck to be brought home in a body bag like a fallen soldier, while all I wanted to do was to come west for a lung full of fresh air and a change of location for a few days.

"Listen," I said to her, when her true intentions became obvious, "in all fairness, I must let you know this, I'm due back at the hospital the day after tomorrow, 'tis the old TB, I'm murdered with it."

She moved so fast away from me, you could hardly see her ass with the flying dust.

"People are faithful for all sorts of reasons," I murmured to old Jack.

He nodded in agreement, he always did.

"For the love of God man, let's get up to the bar and I'll buy you a drink."

I was growing uneasy. Jack heard that alright.

And my God, did we leather out De Banks and The Rocks of Bawn and The Fields of Athenry when the black porter hit the spot, and to be fair to the Blue Rinse outfit they joined in on the hilarity when they were sufficiently lubricated.

"Psychosomatic."

That's what Jack said my illnesses were when he was able to draw his breath.

I nodded at him, for a change!

I had been a captive member of the Golden Brigade for two nights now and my body was hankering for release – if not fresh air. So, on the third day (biblical), I left the Brigade to attend to their bunions and away with me in the taxi to the salty waters and the open beach. The big sun in the sky was showering Croagh Patrick with its warm beams as we passed merrily by; my suntan oils and togs safely tucked away in my carry bag and the hotel-packed lunch ready for the hungriest man in all Mayo.

"Drop me at the beach just around the bend."

I was glad I left the car behind, for in this way I could saunter into a public house later on and have a scoop or two, if the desire hit me.

I paid my driver. As he sped away, I lifted my head towards the blue sky and wondered was He looking down on me? With the thought still flickering about in my head, I made my way slowly towards the beach – not another soul in creation was there to greet me. I threw my towel on the powdery beach and stared out at the mysterious water. There is nothing I love more, in this life, than to gaze at the ocean; be it day or night; winter or summer. If my spirit could reside somewhere by the sea in the next life, I'd settle for that. I gazed down at the packed lunch but it was far too early to attack that, I had some more thinking to do before I felt entitled to muck into the beautiful grub. I remembered the old stories about the healing power of the salty water of the sea – Jez maybe I'll give it a go. The neurologist said there was no cure for neuropathy. I double-checked that statement on the Internet and no one in cyberspace was holding out much hope of a cure, in my lifetime at least. Now the few gallons of Beamish worked a treat, but it unfortunately was the same old story of using a hammer to crack a nut – the drink worked by neutralizing the entire body and when one emerged from the comatose state, the bloody neuropathy attacked with a renewed vigour, as if it felt outwitted by the drink. So I looked again at the water and decided to force my frame into the bathing togs. I felt conscious of my avoirdupois, even though the beach was as empty as a midnight graveyard. I thought the gulls were screeching louder at me, but that was probably my imagination. Eventually I reached the water and even though the sun was pelting my bald head, the water was freezing – I could have been paddling around the North Pole. If my legs were numb before I ventured into the water, they were practically ceasing up now – Jez, I thought, we could do with a bit of Global Warming around these parts. I gazed out to the horizon and thought of Neptune – the God of the Sea, and when I turned back to the shore, all faraway thoughts drained from me, as I saw a monstrosity of a dog tearing away at my packed-lunch. From a distance, he looked as if he was a member of the Rottweiler Community, so I was OK with him eating my lunch

– if it had been a Yorkshire terrier, I would have killed the fucker on the spot.

I was reluctant to leave the icy waters and face down the beast on the beach. But very soon a man, dressed in a kaki jacket and trousers, appeared on the scene. He looked as if he might be the owner of the dog – who by now had devoured not only my lunch, but half my towel by the look of things. He shouted something at the dog, which to my untrained ear, appeared to be in German.

He has come all the way from Germany and it would be my luck, for the beast to find my packed lunch, on the loneliest beach in the entire continent of Europe. The dog obeyed the orders – just like all Germans – and returned to the owner's side.

I was still reluctant to leave my watery station, least he wanted me for desert. The owner shouted more orders at me, and I, like the beast, instantly obeyed – there is something about that language that makes one automatically respond. Gingerly, I made my way to the beach and slowly moved towards the war scene. The dog handler was moving in the same direction, but thankfully had the chain firmly secured round the neck of the offending creature. As we moved closer, I could see the see the dog licking his lips, after devouring the tastiest packed-lunch he had ever laid eyes on. The owner of the beast was a middle-aged man with a tuft of blond hair sweeping across his head and a devilish twinkle in his eye.

"Sorry about the dog," he called out in my direction.

"Never mind," I said, "there's plenty more where that came from."

It was easy to be polite with the monstrosity glaring into your eyes.

"Look," he said.

"I have some towels above in the jeep, let me put this fellow into prison there and I will return with the towels in a few minutes."

And he did.

I dried myself; we exchanged a few words about the dog, who was the gentlest creature one could lay eyes on – he assured me. I believed him and he invited me back to his restaurant for a bite to eat, if I did not mind sharing the journey with the offending beast.

By now the idea of food was winning hands down and off we went in his jeep. I even managed a rub or two for Satan – the dog's name – who, I was assured by the owner, was now firmly secured behind a steel grill. As we moved along through the beautiful countryside, I thought that already this day, I met God in the sky and Satan on the ground, and who knows what the rest of the day might bring . . .

I had a nice lunch with Gunter and his lovely wife. I downed a few glasses of wine and my attitude changed regarding Satan. He picked up on my change of heart and he pulled his massive frame over beside me and we soon became the best friends in all of Connacht. And it was with a heavy heart, that I said farewell to him, when Gunter drove me back to the hotel. As I bade farewell to my new friend and alighted from the jeep, I could see members of the Golden Brigade making their way back from their ramble, all now in single file like some kind of retreating soldiers returning from a war. They looked in a terrible condition.

Me, now fortified by the Gunter's vino, moved gracefully past the porter and collected my key and headed towards my room.

What a shock awaited me.

There was the outline of a woman in my bed and she had her head covered up. It's that bloody 'Husky One', I thought, is she ever going to leave me alone.

"For the love and honour of the Almighty, would you ever get out of my bed or will you force me to go to the porter to have you ejected?"

Not a move, not a murmur.

Jez, I hope she's not dead, that would land me in right pucker. I pulled at the covers and my heart nearly stopped.

"Would you relax, you bloody eejit, 'tis only me."

It was the wife.

"Well that's the second time today I nearly got a heart attack, what in heaven's name brought you down here?"

She informed me that she had planned this move for a long time and had come to Westport by train, and informed the hotel people that she wanted to surprise me.

She certainly did that!

We had an amorous encounter; I forgot my neuropathy; I told her about Satan and Gunter and his wife and the Husky One who tried to seduce her husband. I told her that when I returned to Dublin I would be the most 'Intriguing House Husband' for miles around – for that's what the Golden Brigade thought I was. She said I was the barmiest man about and getting worst by the day.

That night we dined in Westport in the most beautiful restaurant, and the sun slanted through the windows, and we talked about dreams, and mad things we wanted to do, and how by some miracle we managed to get to this point in our lives, and what the future had in store for us. And as we lingered on for hours in the restaurant, we could very easily be on our honeymoon again, for time, like the sun, had fallen away on that beautiful evening.

CHAPTER FIFTEEN

The next morning, the wife and myself headed east and left behind the Golden Brigade on the sun soaked western shore. I was heading home, like a man that had just captured Everest – I felt that good. I had gone to Westport, at the instigation of my wife, with the sole objective of lifting my spirit and in doing so to banish the black dog from my shoulders and out my life. I was returning home with a triumphant air, as if I had achieved something very important. While all I did, was to potter about in a hotel with a bunch of old fogies for a few days; but somehow, getting away from Dublin and the four walls of the house, helped work the oracle. First of all, on my return home, I was going to abandon the title of 'House Husband' irrespective of what the insurance company says. If I have to pay an extra couple of quid for insuring my car from now onwards for changing my status to artist – so be it. It was about time I restored a bit of pride and dignity to my life.

'The value you put on yourself is the value the world puts on you.'

When most people of my age are thinking of buying a new furry pair of slippers, or are trying to figure out how to put a sailing ship into a glass bottle, I was planning something very interesting and risky to life and limb. I was planning to do poetry readings in the pubs of Dublin, and if I should survive that ordeal I was then embarking on my new career as a motivational speaker. Having jumped a few hurdles myself, I would be in the perfect place to lend a hand to others out there in the big bad world. The family was behind me and said I was born for the front of stage life. I somehow got the feeling that they just wanted me out of the house and if I suggested to them that I was taking up ballooning, or perhaps formula one racing, they would have been just as enthusiastic. After a week of reflection, I made a few probing phone calls to friends and acquaintances and I eventually secured my first gig. Some people in the Temple Bar area of Dublin were holding a cultural evening – an excuse for a booze up – and as I was the only living poet who asked for the gig I was given the onerous task of opening proceedings. Now you may be aware, that the pub is not the ideal venue for poetry – the clientele tend to be more interested in the taste of the pint or the price of the half one – but I reckoned, if I could cut my teeth in these types of venues, the National Concert Hall would be a piece of piss after that.

I put my head firmly on the block when I chose Humour as my theme for my part of the proceedings. As I was first up on stage, I reckoned that I had some chance of making an impact and holding the audience, before the demon drink kicked in with the crowd. My stint went down very well – in fact the bloody thing was a rip roaring success and it was with some reluctance that the audience let go of me. But in the end, I had to make way, so that the traditional story teller from the west could take the stage.

I was hooked!

The buzz I got from the whole encounter was overwhelming.

Why the fuck haven't I being doing this all the time, instead of wasting away my life tied to the shagging house. I never felt more relevant or alive – it was almost a spiritual experience. Could it be possible, that I waited sixty years to discover my true calling? Now I always knew I was slow starter, but this was ludicrous.

And I got paid for it as well.

When I returned home, the wife thought I had been to hypnotist; I was on such a high.

"Whatever you got tonight," said the wife, "I could do with some of that myself."

My seventeen and a half stone frame, even felt lighter, and it was the first time in yonks that I did not have a single pain in my body. When I mentioned this to the wife, she said she could understand how poetry might be uplifting to the mind, but the body was another story.

"It was the act of performing I informed her; not the poetry per se."

If I had been reciting the Ten Commandments it would have been the same, it was the feeling of entertaining and that wonderful feeling of power. Getting outside of your own skull and into someone else's. The wife half agreed, and as the night was drifting on, she headed for the scratcher and left me with my mug of tea and a head floating with ideas and ambitions. Three mugs later, I was still hatching plans for the future, as I listened bewitched, to the haunting music of Mozart's 'Eine Kleine Nachmusik. The music finally washed over my thoughts and brought me to that mellow place, where the soul is at rest and the world does not seem a bad place after all. Happy in my skin I surrendered to the gentle sleep of the night.

I woke at six to the chorus coming from the back garden; the sun was edging around in the sky and positioning itself to shine through my window. I was still buzzing from the happenings of the previous evening.

'The first day of the rest ...'

I hurried into the kitchen to make breakfast. Instinctively I prepared fresh orange juice, retrieved the cereal box from the back of the cupboard and left the rashers and sausages at rest in the fridge. The wife appeared at the table, never mentioning the non-appearance of the rashers; I switched on the radio.

"Relax and enjoy life in the realization that all you need to know will be revealed in perfect sequence in time and space."

The voice disappeared.

"That was the thought for the day," the radio announcer proclaimed.

Leaning over my cornflakes, I repeated the entire sentence as if it had been in my head since I first drew my first breath on this planet.

"Relax and enjoy life …"

"I'll go," I shouted.

"You'll go where?" said the wife, a perplexed look on her face.

"To America."

"My goodness, but that's a sudden change of heart."

My nephew was getting married, in Albany upstate New York and my wife had pleaded with me to make the trip to the wedding. But I had refused, point blank, to go, for fear of getting ill on the journey. It was going to be the trip of a lifetime, with twenty two of my family members flying out from Shannon, and many others flying there from the four corners of the globe. It was going to be bigger than Mecca.

"Do you know something; I will make it a belated sixtieth birthday present."

Another problem resolved.

"Upwards and onwards then, America here I come," I shouted.

"Shouldn't that be Philadelphia here I come?" the wife corrected.

With just two weeks to go to lift-off, we gathered the money for the airline tickets and my nephew arranged the hotel accommodation in America. With my new found energy and verve for life, I went about researching America as if I was planning an invasion of that country. By the end of the first week I could have reproduced a map of the eastern side of America straight out of my head; such was the thoroughness of my research. My poetry readings had to be put on ice for the present.

'A ship is safe in a harbour but it was not made for that.'

Wise words that were stored and trapped in my cranium for years were finding expression. I had experienced a new kind of freedom, when I at last confronted my fears and decided to travel to America. My metamorphous was truly under way and what better place to start my new life of freedom than in the great USA – the irony was not lost on me!

Having dispatched our beloved mutt in Blackrock, we joined the motor cavalcade out of Cork the following morning and headed for Shannon. The pilgrims were in a buoyant mood, full of expectancy as to what they might find at the other side of the pond. Six or seven hours later we were heading for JFK airport, and low and behold my heart hadn't stopped on the flight nor had my leg fallen off, so I assumed that once the plane landed OK, I would probably survive for another day. My two nephews were waiting for us in the airport and we were quickly ushered to the black SUV's – we could have been in Chicago in the twenties.

Albany, here I come!

The traffic on the highways brought me back to that fateful day in Paris when I had to drive that shagging camio around the Arc de Triomphe, and I was glad I was not behind the wheel on those bloody highways of America. Two hours later and Roy Rogers was serving me up a skyscraper of a burger and bucket of coke. I felt like a true American already. Jez if I kept eating those size meals I would need an American troop carrier to get me back to Shannon. On reaching Albany, I adjusted the watch on my wrist but I could not adjust the clock in my head – I was whacked. A few beers in the hotel bar finally nailed me and as soon as I hit the pillow the room spun around a few times and I ascended once more into the clouds; this time without the plane. When I eventually woke, the wife had a frown on her face that would frighten Genghis Khan; she was dressed and reading the breakfast menu.

"Is America not suiting you then?"

I asked with a soft voice.

"It's your snoring ... it's a wonder you were not arrested for disturbing the peace last night – I didn't get a wink of sleep with you."

"Look, it was the flight and the time difference and all the movement ... and the jet lag ... I'll be more settled tonight."

"You'll be dead if you gave a repeat performance."

She was always inclined to exaggerate.

"Look, I'll hit the shower, and in ten minutes I'll be ready to grab America by the arse."

When we reached the lobby my eyes nearly dropped out of their sockets – the place was buzzing. The Baptist Convention, I was informed by the big banner over the reception area, was about to be held in the hotel. The entire flock in the lobby was black and wore the most fantastic clothes. The men were decked out in dark suits and gleaming white shirts and they wore the loudest ties this side of the equator. The women mostly wore daffodil-yellow suits and hats that any bird would be proud to call his nest. They were smiling at everyone and everything and flashed sparkling white teeth as if they were all in competition for the Macleans ad. In all my days roaming this planet I have never encountered a happier bunch of people.

I thought of my own life, while resting in the lobby, and how the last few weeks had been the best in over thirty years. My illness's had been put on the back burner and while I still had to take my medication each day by the bucket-load, I had a far happier disposition. America was going to be my new experience and I was about to imbibe every precious moment of it. I had procrastinated and postponed trips for years, due to fear, but at last I was on American soil and the sight before my eyes in the lobby reminded me that I was far from Goleen Town Hall. Over the following days, I got friendly with the brethren, they even managed to flog me one of those spectacular ties that reached all the way down to my knees, but the wife put an instant ban on me wearing it. Our family and friends were arriving at the hotel for the wedding, from all parts of the globe, on a daily basis and some of the brethren must have thought that we were holding our own convention. And our group all dined together each evening, which made for a great gathering and magnificent banter. One evening, while eating at Smokey Bones, both my nephews ordered twenty–two ounce steaks and when the waiter asked what way they would like them; one smartass replied to just cut off the tail and wipe the arse.

Now you would not hear the brethren speak in those tones!

The great party, prior to the wedding, was held in a golf club on the outskirts of Albany. On my way to the party, I got a glimpse of my first field in America – three days after arriving – up to this I thought America was just made up of cities and highways – for that was all I had seen. But there was living proof before my eyes. The in-laws came from proud Italian stock and seeing the assembled spread of food on display, it was easy to identify Italian genius for preparing food. If the Italians have a genius for preparing food, the Irish have a genius for eating food. So we tucked in, and we tucked in, and then we looked for deserts and scoffed them and soon the chocolate fountain came under pressure. If it had been an Olympic event we would have taken gold, silver and bronze that night. During all this time the band – Hair of the Dog – were blasting out Irish songs in one almighty effort to keep us singing and away from the grub. When we hit the Guinness the band realised that we had now lost our yearning for home (with the Guinness, we thought we were home) so they switched the music to sixties and seventies songs. Being on another continent, I forgot I had bad legs, so I led it the charge onto the floor on more than one occasion. The band played with such gusto throughout the evening, that I thought we would be requesting oxygen for them; but they were hale and hearty men with the Celtic blood traipsing through their veins and they survived the rigors of the night. We could not leave without a song or two and the sun was thinking of rising as we left the club, tired and hoarse but happy. Our American driver suggested that we get lessons on how to enjoy ourselves. Even though we were well fortified the irony was not lost on us. We also were aware that there is only one lap in life!

The wedding was held in a traditional Catholic Church. It reminded me of St. Mary's, Popes Quay Church in Cork. When I was but a slip of a boy, my father would take me there every Sunday afternoon for evening devotions. The wonderful aroma of incense wafting round the church in Albany brought me back to those far–off days. The priest gave my nephew plenty of opportunities to make a run for it, by asking him on three occasions if he wanted to go ahead with the wedding, but stoically he held his nerve and the ceremony moved on, much to the relief of the parents who had forked out millions for their outfits. Dominic played the trumpet and the music danced on the high ceilings and on the walls while the deliberate and evocative sound of the organ just below the trumpet filled every square inch of the church. We gave a repeat performance at the wedding reception, as at the party, but this time without the choral work. After shaking hands with half the population of North America I was only fit for bed and I duly dispatched my body to that august setting before the cock crew for the first time. My first duties completed I was aching for pastures new. With the nephew well and truly hitched it was time to say adieu to Albany but not without a disaster. On the night before we were due to travel on to Philadelphia, we decided to go to the pub next door to the hotel for a final drink. The barman introduced me to Grey Goose Vodka when I said I was fed up to the back teeth with the flat beer. Now this barman had no control of his right hand when he poured drink, and after three of the above mentioned Grey Gooses, I thought I was President of America. After another two, I knew I was President of America. When I woke up the following morning my tongue was glued to my palette, my head was throbbing, my neck was as rigid a steel bar and there was sweat oozing out of every pore in my body. My wife had long deserted the room (loyal is right) and I cursed the barman, I cursed the Grey Goose and every Goose in North America.

'Philadelphia here I come.'

With the biggest shit head that any man ever carried on his shoulder.

The hair of the dog ... the hair of the dog fast. The bartender in the hotel in Philly thought I was a demented Irishman as I shouted at him to fetch me a drink as quickly as possible. I was in a life and death situation. It took about four pints of beer and three pint glasses of water before I could straighten my neck. The sad fact was that I never put a short to my lips in Ireland, and in a few short days America had me on my knees. At this rate, and if I had a mind to stay on in the country, I could be a hobo by Christmas. But I soon gathered the reins once more and eased my way back to the land of the living, just by sipping a few harmless beer bottles for the remainder of the day.

Someone once told me many years ago, that the one difference between Ireland and America was that everything worked perfectly well in America all the time, and in my naivety I believed them. The Big Bus Company in Philadelphia blew that idea totally out of the water. The wife (ever by my side) and my two sisters decided to go on a tour of the city and we made our way to the terminus to pick up the bus. Now I have been on buses in Ireland that spluttered and farted their way round Dublin and Cork poisoning the people as they went on their merry way, but I was never on a bus in Ireland where I was exposed to contracting pneumonia. Five minutes into the tour the rains came. Now the Big Bus Company in its generosity, gave us ponchos for fear we might encounter rain when we left the bus – we never in a million years thought we would be wearing them inside the bus. It started with a tingle on my bald head, and I, thinking that some insect might have taken a liking to the Irish skin, lifted my hand to give him the push-off. The tingle turned out to be a drop of rain, which by now was gathering momentum – soon it was pouring all over us. Our host in the bus welded to his microphone, continued with his spiel, totally unaware that we were witnessing the beginning of Second Great Flood. But eventually he had to interrupt his flow when the rain now began to attack him.

"Listen," he says

"Let me apologise for the rain."

"Never mind the rain," I shouted.

"Apologise for the fecking bus."

"Is that an Irish voice I hear," he called out on his microphone.

"Now, we are approaching a house that will mean a great deal to any Irish person."

The weather was forgotten.

"On my left is where Grace Kelly was born."

He went on with his stories about Grace and for a moment or two we forgot about the rain. No one else in the bus was complaining so I shut up as well. By the time we reached The Liberty Bell the sun was raging in the sky and drying out the soaked passengers by the second. If we did not pick up a serious illness from this trip it would be a miracle befitting of Lourdes. The bus showman just carried on reminding us that Philadelphia was once the capital on the United States and we saw where the first post office operated from, and where the first medical operation was performed – I was glad I was not about at that time.

Any man who uttered so many memorable lines in his lifetime deserves to have a bridge named after him. And in addition to uttering those lines he was a scientist, inventor, statesman, printer, philosopher, musician and economist. The Benjamin Franklin Bridge is a true testament to the scope and range of this extraordinary American. Looking up at the Bridge that spans The Delaware River from the thirty-second floor of our hotel was an awesome sight, as the little dinky cars snake their way to and fro – their flickering lights puncturing the night's darkness. Philadelphia is Benjamin Franklin terrain – his name is on everything and never did a man deserve it more. He was a man in touch with the creative side of his being and he had lost the fear of being wrong very early on in his life. On my research I discovered that we were both born on the seventeenth of January – I was hoping that some of Old Benji's creativity might rob off on me during my visit.

Tempus fugit!

Soon it was time to fill up the black SUV's once more and wave goodbye to Mr. Franklin and The Big Bus Company and the monsoons and the ponchos as we pointed in the direction of Washington. The circus was rolling again.

'Philadelphia there I go.'

But I promised to return to old Philly one day, for I liked the homely feel about the place and felt very much at home there.

As we scooted down the highway, I thought about home, probably for the first time since I left for the great US of A. Were the gigs coming thick and fast?

There is nothing wrong with dreaming.

And after all, I had plenty of time to organise once I got home – relax and enjoy.

Washington was wonderful basking in the sunshine – the center of power on the planet. When I heard about the long walk from Capitol Hill down to the Lincoln Memorial I grabbed the air shoes straight away. I need not have bothered, for as soon as I hit the Air and Space Museum I was hooked for the day. It would be the next day before I would parade down the National Mall and walk all the way to the Lincoln Memorial. Just like Martin Luther King, I stood on those steps high above the Mall and imagined all those hundreds of thousands of people that assembled there all those years ago . . .

'I have a dream ...'

I can still remember the day.

And I have a dream myself; for this is a good place to have a dream.

Arlington cemetery brought Shakespeare to mind. Standing beside the grave of J.F. Kennedy I remembered the lines from Henry IV:

'When that this body did contain a spirit

 A kingdom for it was too small a bound;

 Now two paces of the vilest earth

Is room enough.'

I looked back through the trees at the White House in the distance and I remembered the man, who stood not ten feet away from me, on that famous visit to Ireland. Now, he was lying at my feet.

Sic transit gloria mundi.

With a little tear welling up in my socket, I made my way with the rest of the pilgrims to the Tomb of the Unknown Soldier. I wondered who he might be – could he be an Irishman; there probably was a good chance, for the cemetery displayed an amazing number of Irish names on the headstones. We just got there in time for the start of the changing of the guard ceremony and we took our places, with a hundred others, to watch the pageant unfold. The characters in Madame Tussauds looked more human than the lot I saw parading that day, make no mistake they were all battery controlled. When the deed was done and the guards were changed, we dragged our weary legs and limbs to the train and headed for Georgetown for another of those Last Supper dinners. Our last night in Washington – we made it a good one and taxied back to the university where we were holed up for the duration of our trip.

New York, New York!

It was beckoning and the SUV's were on their way.

The university sent us on our way with just a cup of coffee and a croissant so the call of Roy Rogers – the take-away kid – was high on the agenda as we motored down the highway. A king-sized burger in Roy Rogers looked more like a foundation for a semi-detached house but believes me, it had an unbeatable taste. However 'An rud is annamh is iontach' and if it contained an extra calorie or a thousand what the hell, weren't we on our holidays anyway. From my perch, high up on the SUV, I was goggled-eyed looking at the number of trucks on the highway and it was this fact, above everything, else that helped me come to terms with the vast size and scale of this country. I knew I would be adjusting again when I hit Manhattan for the first time.

As we rolled along down the highway from Washington the spirits were high with anticipation, and eventually New York came out to meet us. I did not envy my nephew at the wheel but he was coolness personified, as he maneuvered his way over bridges and under tunnels as traffic came at him from all directions. After what I thought was a white knuckle trip we arrived at our destination.

New York, New York, I came to see you at last.

And we were as lucky as hell, for they had built Time Square only five minutes away from our hotel. The dapper little hotel porter was all decked out in a shocking red coat and black pants and wore white gloves to compliment the outfit. But he belied his persona, for he was as strong as an ox, and he quickly had our gear all stacked away in the lobby, and had his hand firmly pointed in our direction expecting a fistful of dollars. When I delivered the tip to the outstretched paw, the frown on his face suggested that he was not a happy bunny – I was annoyed by his ingratitude and commented aloud that he probably wanted the deeds of my house as well.

He heard the comment and shot off like a shuttlecock weaving his way round the great mountain of luggage. We had no sooner dispatched our luggage when that word was mentioned: the most dreaded word in the male lexicon – SHOPPING! Before I was incorporated into the shopping expedition, I am ashamed to admit, that I was forced to fall back on an old defense mechanism –

My Health!

I had vowed to myself that that I would not mention the word under any circumstances in America even if my leg dropped off on the sidewalk. But every man has his breaking point –

And shopping … And shopping with a bunch of women …

I needed to lie down badly!

The bunch was sympathetic and said that I was great to endure such a rigorous schedule without a murmur of protest. The taxi took the shoppers away in a euphoric state and I stuck myself in the corner of the lobby with the New York Times. The chair was almost a bed and just as comfortable; and by page four of the paper I was fast asleep. So much for the excitement of the Big Apple.

That evening the shoppers returned; my wife had bought a few tops – well enough to last her until 2080.

"They're practically giving the stuff away," she gasped.

"Wait 'til your visa bill arrives, you might discover that they are not quite so generous."

"You should have come along; they had fantastic jumpers for men."

"Look," I said.

"I have more jumpers than Oxfam; I don't need to buy another stitch."

By now the wife was wading through her purchases and was so taken up with the task she forgot that I was in the room, so I humped off to the shower.

The bright lights of New York were waiting for me!

Where is the last place in the world you would expect to find a baldy, fat, over sixty-year old man?

In the Hard Rock Café in Times Square, of course.

Yes, that is where we headed to celebrate our first night in New York. I peered at the memorabilia that festooned the walls to see if there was any photo of myself on the old BSA Gold Flash, but I'm afraid that history did not capture those immortal days of me in London. When we were watered and fed in that august café, we left in some hurry to extradite ourselves from the loud music. Goggle-eyed from the flashing lights, dizzy from side-stepping Japanese tourists on the sidewalk, and burdened down from having consumed a half hundred-weight of fries (chips to you and me) and monster–sized beef burgers.

And we still had to catch up with the rest of the pilgrims who had taken themselves off to the Irish boozer earlier on in the night. There was a great atmosphere in the pub, but as the night wore on the whole saga was taking its toll on me. The body that had stayed loyal to me throughout the trip to America was beginning to complain, and I knew in my heart I had come to the end of my tether. So before the night had really got into full swing, I skedaddled back to the hotel and hit the sack. I needed the next day to recover and just hung around the hotel while the energetic bunch explored New York.

By day three I had recharged the old batteries and headed off to Ground Zero, took the boat to Liberty Island, marvelled at the Lady, felt sad in Ellis Island and returned for our Final Last Supper in Manhattan. And as the music was rising and the dancing on the pier was beginning, I looked out at the waters and my eye stretched further to Liberty Island and sideways towards Ellis Island and I remembered the millions of Irish who floated on these very waters; their hearts pumped up at the thought of a new life in the great Land of the Free. Their journey just beginning, ours just finishing. I raised a glass to the sky and saluted their courage and their lives.

The odyssey in America was over.

Tomorrow we would turn our noses once more in the direction of the Emerald Isle.

There was still a great deal for me to discover in New York but that was for another day.

And as we boarded the plane at JFK, I promised to return in the spring. A meal, a few glasses of vin rouge, a great deal of banter and we were back in Shannon once more.

Home, sweet home … but absolutely knackered!

CHAPTER SIXTEEN

On arriving home, I was so tired and sleepy I could have been bitten by the tsetse fly on my travels. America had been fantastic, but it had also taught me a lesson, that I needed to pace myself from now onwards. Albany, Philadelphia and Washington had drained me, and even though the spirit was willing when I reached New York, the tank was pretty empty. Now with my new phase in my life about to unfold, it was imperative that I now pace myself at all times. I made a few calls to let the natives know that the prodigal son had returned, and would be back in circulation after getting forty-eight hours continuous sleep. The wife was so excited about her shopping, she forgot she was tired. Having served my self-imposed quarantine for a week, I let myself loose onto the streets of Dublin once more. My first exercise was to write to all my medical consultants and doctors and to cancel all appointments for six months; I was still resolute about taking my medication – keeling over in the street was not one of my ambitions. For three weeks I could not get a sausage – no readings, no creative writing classes and certainly no motivational speaking seminars. The world had forgotten about me while I was spinning around America, but the darkest hour is just before dawn and the phone rang.

Ten creative writing classes?

Was I interested?

I was up and running.

"Relax and enjoy life, in the realization that all you need to know will be revealed in perfect sequence in time and space."

I needed to get that statement printed and hung on my wall. Shortly afterwards I got a call to do some poetry readings, and while things were in no way snowballing, I had a positive feeling that everything was turning out as I had planned. Reaching sixty had been a very positive thing for me, beating the nasty neuropathy along with my other little difficulties was going to be another huge challenge. With the jet lag and the tiredness now well and truly gone from my system, I got a great surge of energy from the whole experience in America. I had broken the fear that I was unable to travel on a plane for more than four hours without returning home in a body bag, and this was a huge fillip for me in going forward and confronting the other demons that were waiting for me around every street corner. If I allocated two weeks for my work and two weeks for other activities it might introduce some balance and thereby remove the possibility of overstretching myself. One thing was certain, there had to be a huge space for fun and half-mad ideas in my life, for that was my best way of coping – be I six or sixty.

'Turning every minute upside down and inside out for the fun that's in it,' had to be still my mantra. For if I was pre-occupied with all the stuff that had be-fallen me, and if I allowed each and every event to impinge on my life, I would end up in the nuthouse. Perhaps this was my natural home.

Almost unbeknownst to myself, as I was sheltering behind the four walls of the house and pondering about my own illnesses over the previous fifteen years, a big revolution was happening in Ireland. The entire fabric of Irish society was changing rapidly, and the new entrants to Ireland were adding a colourful and rich tapestry to the landscape. This was very evident in the creative writing classes. They brought originality, wonderful colour, and a rare freshness to the subject of writing. In my classes the predominant features of all the immigrants was their desire to learn and share ideas. For me, it was a whole new learning experience also, as I listened to the many stories of Africa, Poland, Romania and the many other countries that exported their flock to our green and misty shores. Most writers were telling their stories in a second language and I could empathise with their difficulty after my experiences in Paris. This phase in my life was turning out to be the most exciting and rewarding time since my twenties. Because the classes were so successful, and because I was engaged in something I truly loved, my self-esteem rose to unprecedented heights. My new found positivity was seeping into other areas of my life. The air shoes were glued to my feet as if there were a permanent feature, the line to Tony Robbins was open at all times and I was meditating like a Tibetan monk. The waistline had given up its expansionist role and was settling down round the forty-four mark. The hair refused to make a re-appearance on the head, but one cannot expect everything in life. Around this time something else happened – I began to read again. I was prepared to open my mind once more to the big bad world. In my younger days I was an avid reader, and by the time I was thirty years old had served my time reading the Russian masters; now again I began to read everything and anything, and I stumbled across the Genome Project. In 2003, when the world was first hearing the magnificent news that the scientists in London and America had mapped the genetic make-up of a human being for the first time, I was probably experimenting with some kind of new medication; either way I did recall hearing it at the time; or if I did, the immense significance of it did not register with me. Now, reading about it a few years later, I am convinced they did all that work just for me. Imagine now, that just by altering a few genes here and there, they were able to cure my gout, heal my neuropathy, lower my blood pressure, reduce my cholesterol, throw a few inches on to my height, bring my weight under control, grow a new crop of hair on my head, and smoothen out the rough patches on my skin – I could live for another sixty years. Imagine if they could do all this, without me having to take a single tablet or portion, and the whole lot could be done without an overnight stay in any hospital. Imagine if they could do that … they will!

They have the technology; all they need to do now are the sums.

If they do their sums in time, I may be still roaming the planet in 2100 and healthier than I am today.

'Hope springs eternal …'

I was telling my creative writing class about the aforementioned scenario and Sergio disappeared from the class and eventually returned with a glass of water.

"Take these, and lie down for a few minutes and you will be okay."

We all laughed.

Sergio got his point across; he was well aware, in spite of his young age that he was dealing with a complete lunatic. But it provided me with a great opportunity to point out that everything begins with a dream. The great books, the great paintings and the mind-boggling inventions all began because someone dared to dream.

And the wonderful news is that we can dream at any age.

Maybe the whole thing is a dream.

Prospero:

Our revels now are ended. These our actors,
As I foretold you, were all spirits, and
Are melted into air, into thin air:
And like the baseless fabric of this vision,
The cloud-capp'd tow'rs, the gorgeous palaces,
The solemn temples, the great globe itself,
Yea, all which it inherit, shall dissolve,
And, like this insubstantial pageant faded,
Leave not a rack behind. We are such stuff
As dreams are made on; and our little life
Is rounded with a sleep.

Someone once posed the question, as to how we know that this world is not another man's hell … he was probably having a bad day at the time.

However, we are here with the great mystery and the great unknown, on the great journey we call Life!

www.ingramcontent.com/pod-product-compliance
Lightning Source LLC
Chambersburg PA
CBHW051947220626
47052CB00004B/826